"Joey needs his father. You're his father. Not me. Not someone you hire from an agency, but you."

Gina continued, "My terms are simple. Joey has six weeks of the summer holiday ahead of him. You've got to make use of that time. You learn sign language. Talk to him. And listen to him. Plus you leave work early—no more getting home at ten. You take at least a week off to give him a holiday somewhere. I want your solemn word. If I don't get it, I leave this minute."

"You warned me you were tough," he said.

"I had to be. You'll discover that Joey's tough, too."

"If I give you these promises, I want one in return."

"What?"

"That you'll stay with us the whole six weeks. I can do it, Gina, but not without you."

Lucy Gordon cut her writing teeth on magazine journalism, interviewing many of the world's most interesting men, including Warren Beatty, Richard Chamberlain, Roger Moore, Sir Alec Guinness and Sir John Gielgud. She also camped out with lions in Africa, and had many other unusual experiences which have often provided the background for her books.

She is married to a Venetian, whom she met while on holiday in Venice. They got engaged within two days, and have now been married for twenty-five years. They live in the Midlands, U.K. with their two dogs.

Two of her books, *His Brother's Child* and *Song of the Lorelei*, won the Romance Writers of America RITA award, in the Best Traditional Romance category.

Books by Lucy Gordon

HARLEQUIN ROMANCE®
3634—THE SHEIKH'S REWARD
3596—RICO'S SECRET CHILD

Don't miss any of our special offers. Write to us at the following address for information on our newest releases.

Harlequin Reader Service
U.S.: 3010 Walden Ave., P.O. Box 1325, Buffalo, NY 14269
Canadian: P.O. Box 609, Fort Erie, Ont. L2A 5X3

FOR THE SAKE OF HIS CHILD
Lucy Gordon

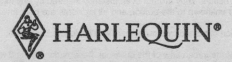

HARLEQUIN®

TORONTO • NEW YORK • LONDON
AMSTERDAM • PARIS • SYDNEY • HAMBURG
STOCKHOLM • ATHENS • TOKYO • MILAN • MADRID
PRAGUE • WARSAW • BUDAPEST • AUCKLAND

ISBN 0-373-03640-X

FOR THE SAKE OF HIS CHILD

First North American Publication 2001.

Copyright © 2000 by Lucy Gordon.

Visit us at www.eHarlequin.com

Printed in U.S.A.

CHAPTER ONE

YOU'RE PERFECT, my darling, do you know that? A bit small, perhaps, but size isn't everything, is it? To me, you're perfect. And you're the love of my life!

Gina came out of her happy dream, and looked around hastily in case she'd spoken her thoughts aloud. But nobody in the car park had noticed her. Relieved, she patted the little car lovingly, and it seemed to shine more brightly, basking in her adoration.

It was, as she'd admitted, tiny. It was also twelve years old and had come at a knock-down price. People had been known to chuckle at the sight of it. But it was hers. It served her faithfully in a chug-chug fashion. And she loved it.

Her smile faded as she tried to open the door to get in. On one side of her was a brick wall. On the other side was a large Rolls-Royce, whose owner plainly felt entitled to take up more than his own parking space. She was tightly hemmed in.

'Now, that's not on,' she muttered. 'I can't even open the door far enough to get in.'

Luckily the car had no barrier between the boot and the seats. By climbing through the back, Gina was able to reach the driver's seat. It was squashed, undignified, and did nothing to improve her temper.

'Who does he think he is?' she muttered.

She began to back out slowly, holding her breath. At first all went well, but suddenly the little car threw a temper tantrum, slewed to the side and slammed into the shiny Rolls with an ugly grating sound.

Horrified, she squeezed out of the back again and went down on one knee to inspect the damage. Both vehicles were badly scratched and dented but on the Rolls it looked worse.

'That was clever,' said an ironic male voice above her head. 'I'd just had it resprayed, too. Ten out of ten for timing!'

From this angle he looked enormous. His head of thick, dark hair towered over her from a great height and his shoulders seemed broad enough to blot out the sun. Hastily Gina got to her feet, but he still had eight inches over her, and it was exasperating to have to express her righteous indignation looking up.

'Clever isn't the word I'd choose,' she said. 'Selfish and arrogant, maybe.'

'Who?'

'Whoever parked this Rolls using two parking spaces, and leaving me no room to get out.'

'Just how much room does this peanut on wheels need?'

'We can't all drive a Rolls,' she said, incensed at this slur on her beloved.

'Just as well. If you drove a Rolls the way you drive this—this—'

'You're encroaching on my space. You didn't even leave me enough room to open the door. You had no right to park like that.'

'Actually, it wasn't me. My chauffeur parked it.'

'I might have known.'

'I see! If owning a Rolls is a crime, having a chauffeur is a hanging offence, right?'

'It's all of a piece, isn't it? Anyone who can afford a

chauffeur doesn't need to think of other people. Why didn't you stop him doing this?'

'Because I wasn't in the car at the time. This is the first I've seen of it, and I'll agree he didn't do a brilliant job. But let's face it. He still left you room to back out, if you'd gone in a straight line. You're not supposed to do a sharp turn, or did nobody tell you?'

'If you'd left me my rightful space,' Gina said crossly, 'I'd still have missed you, no matter how many sharp turns I did.'

'Your steering is defective,' the man said, with exasperated patience. 'And you're damned lucky it came to light now and not when you were trying to avoid a truck.'

He was right, of course. That just made it worse. Now she was faced with a huge repair bill.

'So what shall we do?' the man asked. 'Exchange insurance details, or would you prefer pistols at dawn?'

'This isn't funny—'

'If we make a fight of it, I could say a few things about your wonky steering—'

'Will you stop casting aspersions at my car?'

'Considering what your car has done to mine, aspersions are the least I'd like to cast at it. The insurers will probably declare that little rabbit hutch a write-off.'

'Now, look—'

'So why don't I just accept all the blame and pay for your repairs and mine?'

His sudden capitulation cut the ground out from under her. Her indignation died.

'You'd—do that?'

'Yes, despite my disgraceful chauffeur and my reprehensible Rolls, I have some human qualities after all.'

'Thank you,' she said meekly.

A middle-aged man had approached and was watching the scene. The other man turned to him.

'You've landed me in it, Harry. What were you thinking of to park like this?'

'Sorry, guv, but the bloke on the other side—he's gone now—was taking up half our space, so I thought it wouldn't matter if— Oh, my Gawd!' He'd seen the damage.

'Never mind. Just drive this lady's—er—car to my usual garage and tell them to do what's needed. Then come back here, take the Rolls—dents and all—and drive it to the garage.'

'How do I get in?' Harry demanded.

'Through the back,' Gina said through gritted teeth.

He squeezed into the little car and eased it gingerly out, only just managing not to graze the Rolls again. The man cast Gina a speaking look but maintained a tactful silence.

'I'm sorry,' she said awkwardly.

'It's not your day, is it? Where can we sit down and swap details in comfort?'

'There's a little place over there.'

He looked wildly out of place in Bob's Café, a cramped greasy spoon that catered for people with little money and less time. He must have been a good six foot two, with long legs, broad shoulders and a set to his head that suggested authority. His suit was pure Savile Row, as befitted a man with a Rolls, but his air of confidence was his own.

She cast a disparaging glance down at her own clothes. Her grey business suit was neat and appropriate to her job, but it had been the least expensive in the store. She kept it varied with the clever use of scarves and jewellery, but this man looked as though his normal companions wore haute couture.

She tried to remind herself that he was the villain of the piece, but that was hard when he'd offered to pay all the bills.

It was lunchtime and the place was just filling up, but he found them a window table. He was the sort of man, Gina realised, who would always be able to find a window table in a crowded place.

'Let me buy *you* a coffee,' she suggested. 'It's the least I can do.'

'Forget it. I'd rather heap coals of fire on your head.' He studied the menu. 'I'm hungry and I don't like to eat alone. Choose something.'

'Yes, sir.'

He grimaced. 'Sorry. It's my way. I'm used to giving orders, and it's a hard habit to break.'

His voice was deep and resonant, making her realise that most voices were flat.

She made her choice and he hailed a waitress without trouble. When he'd given the order he said, 'My name's Carson Page.'

'And mine is Gina Tennison. I'm really grateful to you, Mr Page. You were right about my steering. And it shouldn't have been like that because I've just had the car repaired—'

'You should sue the garage. Get yourself a good lawyer.'

'Actually, I am a lawyer.'

'Good grief!'

'Well, it's hard to be a convincing lawyer in a garage full of male mechanics,' she said defensively. 'It doesn't matter how many legal qualifications you have, they still do what they like because they think you're just a silly woman who knows nothing about cars.'

He didn't answer, but his lips twitched.

'Go on, say it,' she challenged.

'Do I need to?'

She broke into laughter, and he joined her. Laughing transformed him, softening the harsh lines of his face. But it vanished quickly. It was almost as though cheerfulness made him uneasy, and he needed to protect himself against it.

In repose, his face was full of tension. His eyes were dark and shadowed, and there were lines of strain around his mouth. This was a man who lived on his nerves, she realised, and she had a sudden feeling those nerves were at breaking point.

It was hard to guess his age. Somewhere in the thirties was as close as she could get. He had a lean body that moved easily, suggesting youth. But he carried an air of gravity as though life had piled cares on to him. It made his brief smile an unexpected pleasure.

'So you're a lawyer?' he said. 'Where do you work? Around here?'

'Yes, I'm with Renshaw Baines.'

'Renshaw Baines? I'm one of their clients. At least, I shall be after a meeting this afternoon.'

'Oh, heavens, I've offended a client!'

'That's a little unfair when I've been at pains not to be offended.'

'But I scratched your Rolls,' she said, aghast.

'Well, I won't tell anyone if you don't. Anyway, you can make up for it by putting me in the picture about Philip Hale, who's going to handle my affairs. I've never met him before. Describe him.'

'Philip Hale,' she echoed carefully. 'Well, he's the

most recent partner—everyone says he's brilliant—you couldn't have a better man—'

'You really do dislike him, don't you?' he asked, easily reading between the lines.

She gave up. 'Yes—no—it's more that he dislikes me—disapproves of me. He thinks I'm a lightweight, and he didn't want to employ me. Mr Page, I'm really not the person you should ask.'

He smiled again, becoming delightful for a moment. 'I wish you could see your face this minute. All right. I'll spare you. Why does he think you're a lightweight?'

'By his standards, I suppose I am. But he can't fault my paperwork. I've done jobs for him that even he had to admit were up to scratch.'

'Paperwork? No dramatic courtroom appearances?'

'No, thank you,' she said hastily. 'I'm quite happy beavering away in the background.'

'Isn't that a bit dull for a young woman?'

'Not for me,' she said earnestly. 'You see, for years I—'

'Go on.'

'No, I'm just burbling away about myself, and I don't know why. I don't normally go on like that.'

'But I'm interested. What happened, "for years"?'

'I was—ill, that's all. And it didn't seem as though I could live a normal life. But now I do. I've got a good job, and my own modest little bit of success, and it's all like a dream to me. You said it must be dull, but I don't find anything in my life dull, because it's more than I ever hoped for.'

He looked at her, intrigued by the light that had come into her face, wondering if he'd really found that rarest of creatures, someone who was contented with her lot.

'What kind of illness?' he asked gently.

But she shook her head. 'That's enough about me. Please, I don't want to say any more.'

To her relief he didn't press the matter. It made her nervous to be talking to Philip Hale's client, even if he had promised to keep her secret.

Gina had fought to study for her legal exams and passed them well. Renshaw Baines wasn't the biggest legal firm in London, but it had a first-class name and could take its pick of applicants. She was proud of her value to her employers.

At twenty-six she was modestly pretty, with reddish hair, a pale skin and a slim, elegant figure. Her one real beauty was a pair of thrilling eyes, with the colour and depth of emeralds.

But few people had seen how lovely she could be. The circumstances of her life had taught her the value of caution and keeping a low profile. At work she dressed quietly, and even at play she didn't splash out. She had a job which gave her a sense of self-worth, plus a boyfriend who was like an old slipper. And she was content.

His mobile rang and he answered it. It was Harry, at the garage.

'They say it's going to take a whole new engine to make that heap of junk roadworthy. And that'll cost.'

'Tell them to do whatever's necessary,' Carson said, without hesitation.

'Look, guv, you don't need to buy that woman a new engine—'

'Just do it,' Carson Page said brusquely, and hung up. 'They're working on your car now,' he told Gina.

'Is it bad?'

'Nothing that can't be fixed.'

'Is it going to cost you a lot?'

He dismissed the subject with a shrug. 'It's history. Leave it.'

'But—'

'I said leave it.' He sounded impatient. 'You'll have your car back in working order, but I should think you could afford a better one if you're a lawyer.'

'I haven't been qualified long, but I suppose I might think of it now.'

'You certainly should, for everyone's sake,' he said gravely, but his eyes were kind.

Impulsively she said, 'You'll probably think I'm crazy but I'll be sorry to say goodbye to my "peanut". It's been a good friend and it's sad to think that I'll go onward and upward while my friend will languish in a scrapyard, waiting to be broken up.'

'Not for a while yet. When the garage has finished with it you'll be able to sell it to someone equally crazy.'

'That's true,' she said, brightening. 'And they might love it as I do.' She tucked into her salad, which had arrived while they were talking, plainly feeling happier now.

Carson watched her in fascination as he munched on his sandwich. Then he turned his inward eye on himself and was incredulous. He prided himself on not being sentimental, but he'd accepted the blame, and the expense, for something that had been only partly his fault.

And why? Because he'd wanted to see her smile. That was the only explanation he could think of. And it wasn't good enough.

Then he'd compounded his own idiocy by spending time in this dump, with a girl who was plainly cuckoo. He had a thousand better things to do than sit here listening to her talk nonsense.

Or did he?

Suddenly his brows contracted and he rubbed his eyes like a man in pain.

'Are you all right?' she asked. 'Do you have a head-ache?'

'No,' he said quickly.

It was true that his head ached, but it did that so often these days that he disregarded it.

'I think you do,' she said.

For a moment he was annoyed at her persistence. He'd said no and that should be the end of it. But her eyes were gentle and concerned and his flare of anger died.

'Perhaps just a little,' he conceded. 'I've got a lot on my plate at the moment.'

She had a kind face, and for a moment he was tempted to tell her about the disasters that threatened to crush him. It might be easy to confide in this charming stranger about the loneliness of his life after the woman he'd once loved had turned out to be a selfish, calculating shrew.

He might even find a way to tell her about the deeper pain of his son, the little boy of whom he'd once been so proud, but who'd become a pitiful, disadvantaged creature. He could feel compassion for the child, and helpless, agonised love, but no pride.

Then he pulled himself together, wondering what he'd been thinking of. It wasn't his way to show weakness in front of anyone, never mind strangers.

Besides, he didn't want to spoil this moment. She was cheeky, and sweet, and fun.

Fun.

He'd almost forgotten what the word meant. But it meant this delightful young woman with her sunny face, laughing ruefully over her idiotic little car, counting her modest blessings. He was glad he'd yielded to the im-pulse to spend a little time with her. It was good to be reminded that there were people who could face the world with a smile.

He looked at his watch and was amazed to find that an hour had slipped away in her company. 'Time for my appointment with Philip Hale. Have you finished?'

'Goodness.' She gulped her coffee in a hurry. 'Can I have a head start? If we arrive together, people will wonder why, and one question will lead to another—'

'And your dark secret will be exposed. All right. I'll give you five minutes. Here's my card, and I've written the garage number on the back. Call them tomorrow.'

'Thank you. And thank you for the lunch.'

'No problem. Good day to you.'

His hand took hers in a brief grip that almost made her gasp. She had a glimpse of long fingers, and a sharp sensation of power flowing between them. Then he released her and nodded a farewell that was almost a dismissal.

She hurried back to her office, feeling bemused. She'd never met a man who sent out so many confusing signals. He was handsome, with dark, speaking eyes, and might have been charming if he'd let himself relax. But that was obviously what he couldn't do. One side of him—the businessman, presumably—had been reminding him of the time he was wasting. He was probably glad to be rid of her.

Carson Page watched Gina until she was out of sight. He had an odd, deflated feeling, as though the sun had just gone in. He rubbed his eyes again, wondering what had come over him to waste an hour over something that could have been sorted out in five minutes.

He pulled himself together. It had been a delightful interlude, like taking a much needed holiday. But now he must return to the real world, and it would be better not to see her again.

Gina found her secretary deep in paperwork. Dulcie was middle-aged, had worked for the firm for over twenty years and took a robustly cynical view of her employers. But she had a soft spot for Gina.

With her first words, she revealed the flaw in Gina's secrecy arrangements.

'Did I see you having lunch with Carson Page in Bob's Café?' she asked.

'Oh, heavens! You didn't tell anyone, did you?'

'Not a soul. If Philip Hale thinks you're trying to pinch his newest acquisition, there'll be hell to pay.'

'I know. Look, Dulcie, this is for your ears alone—'

'Silent as the grave.'

Gina briefly described what had happened, and Dulcie gave a snort of laughter that she hastily smothered.

'You bashed Carson Page's car and lived to tell the tale?' she asked. 'And he's paying for all the repairs? What's your secret?'

'Nothing. He's just a very nice, reasonable man.'

'He isn't,' Dulcie said at once. 'I've got a friend who works for the last firm of lawyers he employed and he's the client from hell. He owns Page Engineering, and I suppose if he wasn't aggressive he couldn't have made it what it is today.'

'Goodness!' Gina exclaimed. '*That* Carson Page? I never dreamed—I mean, I've heard of him.'

He'd created Page Engineering from nothing, fighting off competition ruthlessly, buying up smaller firms, and carving a large share of the market for himself. He was unstoppable. Whatever he touched turned to gold, or so the financial pages insisted.

He was also a bad enemy, driving opponents into the ground. And she'd dented his Rolls.

'You've got to hand it to him as a businessman,' Dulcie conceded. 'But talk about difficult and demanding!' She eyed her young boss significantly. 'But not with you, eh?'

'Oh, stop it!' Gina said, reddening slightly. 'He was just—I don't know—he was a grouch, but a nice grouch. At least, he was trying to be nice, but he was awkward about it, as though he was using muscles that were a bit stiff.'

'That sounds about right. He's not known for overwhelming people with charm. Obviously you made an impression. Play your cards right and you'll be travelling in that Rolls yourself.'

'Nonsense. I'll never see him again. Anyway, I've got my lovely Dan.'

'I could think of many descriptions for your Dan, but lovely isn't one of them,' Dulcie said tartly. 'He's dull, he's limited, you're only dating him because you've known him since the year dot, and he takes you for granted.'

'Well, I take him for granted, too. It's cosy.'

Dulcie muttered, 'Give me patience,' and returned to her work, but only after Gina had made her promise yet again that not a word would pass her lips.

It was true that she'd known Dan since childhood, and was comfortable with him, but what was wrong with that? she thought, a tad defensively. The long years of suffering a crippling disability had left her willing to count her blessings.

She was meeting him that night in a tiny restaurant a couple of miles away. She booked a taxi, then, on impulse, called the garage and asked about her car.

'You're lucky,' the head mechanic told her. 'It's not easy to find a new engine for that make, but for Mr Page we pulled out the stops.'

'Excuse me—did you say a new engine?' she asked faintly.

'Only thing that will do it. New steering, too.'

'But it'll cost a fortune.'

'Well, it's going on his bill, so why worry?'

'Oh, no, I don't want this—'

'Too late. It's in pieces now.'

Dazed, she put the phone down. She needed that new engine, but to owe a stranger so much!

But, of course, Carson Page was a rich man who'd simply bought off trouble because it was quicker that way. She needn't give him a second thought, any more than he would give her a second thought.

CHAPTER TWO

GINA went to change for the evening ahead, slipping off her smart business suit and donning a simple green dress. It was sleeveless but had a high neck against which rested a dainty pendant.

She brushed out her hair and added a little more make-up. Then she was ready.

She was a few minutes late at the restaurant, but there was no sign of Dan. She ordered herself a sherry, and sat waiting, hoping he wouldn't be too long.

'Do you mind if I join you?'

She looked up to see Carson Page standing, regarding her gravely.

'Are you waiting for someone?' he asked.

'Yes, Dan—my boyfriend. He's a little late.'

'Then I'll only stay a moment.' He sat down. 'I just wanted to let you know that your car will be finished the day after next.'

'I know. I called the garage. Mr Page—'

'Carson.'

'Carson, I had no idea you were going to replace the engine. There was no need for that.'

'According to the garage, there was every need.'

'You know what I mean. I want to pay you—not immediately, but in instalments—'

'All right, pay me one day. Now, can we forget this?'

She agreed, with a horrid suspicion that she was boring him. 'How did you know I'd be here?' she asked.

'I was going to drop in at your office, but I arrived

19

just as you were getting into a taxi. So I told my taxi to follow you.'

He ordered himself a drink, and she watched him, trying to tie this man in with the ogre Dulcie had described. 'Difficult and demanding' she could understand. Even when he was being kind, his air of pride and self-will were unmistakable. A bad enemy. A man who expected things done his way, and at once. A disturbing man. An exciting man.

She tried to brush that idea away, but it lurked on the fringe of her consciousness, taking little pot-shots at her more sedate thoughts.

He was different from other men, as a lion was different from kittens. She wished Dan would hurry up and arrive. Something was happening here that was threatening her carefully constructed world, and if she hurried she might still be in time to avoid it.

'What about your car?' she asked, hoping that her voice wouldn't shake and betray her inner confusion.

'It'll be ready by tomorrow.' He looked at the clock on the wall. 'Seven-twenty. What time was your date supposed to arrive?'

'Any time about now,' she prevaricated. Dan should have been there at seven. 'He's very busy.'

'So am I, but if I make a date with a lady I'm punctual.'

'Actually I'm early. I don't expect him until seven-thirty,' she said defiantly.

'If you say so.' His dark eyes warned her not to try to fool him.

'What did you think of Philip Hale?' she asked, valiantly searching for a new topic of conversation.

'He's everything you said. Brilliant—couldn't have a better man—for a limited range. Also the biggest bore in creation. Never says anything once if he can say it ten times.'

She choked into her sherry and put it down hastily, her shoulders shaking.

'Don't smother it,' he advised her. 'Laugh aloud. He isn't here to know.'

'I shouldn't think anyone's ever spoken about him that way before,' she chuckled.

'Nonsense. Everyone who's ever met him must have said something like that as soon as they escaped.'

He hoped she would go on laughing, because her laughter made the sun come out again. But she controlled herself, pressing her lips together, although her eyes still brimmed with fun. He would have to make do with that.

'Anyway, bore or not, I've decided to take him on. I'm seeing him again tomorrow, heaven help me! He's a good lawyer, within his range. Do you have a speciality?'

'Property and commercial law.'

'So you might be doing some of my work?'

There was a noise in the background. Gina leaned forward, frowning. 'Could you repeat that?'

'You might be doing some of my work.' He saw her watching him intently. 'What is it?'

'I'm deaf,' she said simply.

'Nonsense!' he said brusquely. 'You *can't* be.'

Gina's face broke into the happiest smile he'd ever seen.

'Thank you. That's the nicest thing anyone's said to me since—since I went deaf.'

He frowned. 'But you seem to be hearing me quite normally. Are you saying you've been lip-reading all this time?'

'Oh, no. I have a cochlear implant that helps me. I can hear most things, but if there's background noise I sometimes miss a few words.'

Before her eyes he changed. A heaviness seemed to settle over him. 'I see,' he said. 'I never suspected—'

'Why should you? Apart from the odd moment, I'm just like everyone else.'

'Yes, of course. Forgive me. I was just thinking—'

Gina watched him in dismay. She knew exactly what he was thinking. She was used to people who flinched at the word deaf, who couldn't cope with even the thought.

But not this man, surely? She'd been so sure that he was special that she'd admitted her problem without worrying. Now her heart sank at the thought that he might be no better than the others.

The discovery hurt, but she couldn't escape it. There was no mistaking the chill, withdrawn look that had come over his face. He no longer knew what to say to her.

To her relief she saw Dan hurrying towards her, dodging between the tables. 'Darling, I'm so sorry I'm late. Something came up...'

Carson rose quickly. 'I gather this is your date. I won't keep you.' He nodded politely at Dan and walked away.

'Who was that?' Dan asked, kissing her on the cheek.

'Carson Page. I bashed his car.'

'Good grief! *The* Carson Page? Darling, you shouldn't have let him go so easily. He's a big man.'

'No, he isn't,' Gina said with a little sigh. 'He's just like all the rest.'

The next afternoon, the receptionist called to say that there had been a delivery for Gina. Dulcie was deep in correspondence, so Gina went out herself. And that was how she saw Carson Page arriving, accompanied by a little boy of about eight. The child had a pale, intelligent face, and he looked nervous.

Philip Hale arrived, full of an effusive greeting, which Carson returned politely, but with a cool restraint that would have warned a subtler man than Hale.

It was strange, Gina thought, how the child showed no awareness of the conversation going on over his head. Almost as if…

I'm imagining things, she thought, giving herself a little mental shake.

True to his word, Carson gave no sign of recognising Gina, but followed Philip Hale, his hand on the boy's shoulder.

'I wonder what's the matter with that child?' Gina said to the young woman receptionist.

'Poor little kiddie. Tossed from pillar to post. Parents not speaking, using him as a weapon. Apparently, Mr Page is trying to stop his ex having any access to Joey at all.'

'That's wicked!' Gina exclaimed.

Her view of Carson Page took another knock. Obviously his friendliness the day before had been an aberration, and there was something much more unpleasant beneath the surface.

She returned to her office and got down to business. She worked for half an hour, then she leaned back in her chair, yawned and stretched. It was late afternoon and the sun was hot.

'Oh, heavens!'

She'd happened to glance out of her window, overlooking the main road, and something she saw there made her spring to her feet.

'What's that child doing there?' she demanded, aghast.

It was Joey Page. He was wandering in the busy road, apparently oblivious to the furious honks from the motorists around him. As she watched, a car missed him by an inch. The motorist bawled at him, but the little boy merely looked bewildered, as though nothing that was happening to him was real.

'Oh, my God,' she whispered. 'He doesn't know—he can't—'

The next moment, she'd dashed from her office, running across the reception area and out into the street, praying that she would be in time.

There was more honking as she raced into the road and grabbed Joey. He tried to throw her off, but she held on and guided him firmly back to the pavement.

'What were you thinking of?' she demanded breathlessly. 'You could have been run over.'

'Yaaa—yaaa—yaaaah!' he shrieked, glaring at her and wrenching himself free. But behind the childish fierceness Gina glimpsed bewilderment, as though her words were meaningless, and now she was certain about something that had only been a suspicion before. She knelt so that he could see her lips.

'You're deaf, aren't you?' she said slowly.

'Aaaah!' he yelled.

His face was filled with sullen misery. She knew a flare of anger at the man who'd deprived this vulnerable child of his mother.

'Don't go into the road,' she told him, speaking slowly and clearly. 'It's dangerous.' She tried to put her hand on his shoulder.

'Aaaa!' he screamed, thrashing about so wildly that she was almost knocked off balance.

'Joey!' said a voice behind him. 'Stop that!'

Gina looked up to see Carson, frowning. She rose to face him.

'It's no use shouting at him,' she said. 'He can't hear you.'

'Yes,' he said heavily. 'I know he can't.'

He reached for the child's arm. Instantly Joey swung around to face him and let out another yell. He sounded shocking, like a small demented animal, but Gina, standing close to him, could feel that he was trembling violently.

She could have wept for the child. She knew that bewildered frustration that could only find release in rage. Carson's appalled expression now brought back a host of painful memories, and instinctively she put her arms about Joey.

'I'm his father. I'll take him.'

Gina gasped, trying to fight down the wild anger that surged up in her. She almost never lost her temper, but now it rushed away from her, leaving her shaking.

'If you're his father, what were you thinking of to let him wander away like that?' she demanded. 'Don't you know that deaf children are vulnerable on the roads?'

'I don't need to be lectured about my own son,' he snapped.

'I think you do. A father worth his salt would protect this child properly.'

The look he flung her was so full of rage that anyone else might have been intimidated, but Gina was too cross to care. What did this man matter beside the hurt child?

'He's got problems,' she cried. 'He can't hear. That means he needs more love and care, not less. He needs his mother.'

'That's enough!' Carson's face was frozen. 'You

know nothing about it. Perhaps you would be good enough to bring him inside.'

Gina grasped the child by the hand and led him back into the building. To her relief, there was nobody in Philip Hale's office.

'I'm grateful to you for rescuing him,' Carson said, 'and for the trouble you've taken—'

'It's no trouble,' Gina told him firmly. 'I'll get him some—' She stopped and put herself where Joey could see her. 'Milk and chocolate biscuits,' she said, speaking clearly. 'Would you like that?'

He nodded. His expression was still belligerent but, when she tried to leave the office, Joey took a firm hold of her hand. It was as though he'd discovered safety at last, and he wasn't going to risk losing it. Gina called Dulcie on the internal line and asked her to bring the refreshments.

'They'll soon be here,' she told Joey. But he frowned. He hadn't understood.

'They will soon be here,' she said, slowly and with emphasis. This time he nodded, and Gina gave him her most reassuring smile. After what seemed like an age, he managed a half-smile in return, but it was gone at once.

Just like his father, she thought.

He had a round face with well-defined features that were just beginning to reflect Carson's. There was character beyond his years in that face, and mobile eyebrows that suggested a touch of humour. Behind the barrier of deafness a strong personality was developing, Gina thought.

Dulcie entered, and Joey's eyes lit up at the sight of a plate of chocolate biscuits. But before he touched them he looked up at his father. Gina thought she saw apprehension in that glance, and her anger grew again.

'He's afraid of you,' she accused.

'He's afraid of everything,' Carson said wearily.

'Of course he is. When you're deaf, the world is a very scary place, but he should be able to rely on you to help him through it. You're his father; you should stand between him and the things that threaten him.'

'I don't know how!' he snapped. As soon as the words were out, his face closed against her, as though he'd been betrayed into an admission of weakness, and resented her for it.

'He could have got killed out there but you haven't put your arms around him. All you could think of was apologising to me. As though I matter, beside him.'

She checked herself. Out of the corner of her eye she'd glimpsed Philip Hale approaching.

'Why don't I take Joey to my office, so that you can get on with your business?' she said quickly.

'Thank you.'

She faced the child. 'Come along. And we'll take these.' She took the tray with the milk and biscuits, and they went out together.

Luckily Gina found her office empty, which would give her time to talk to Joey and ease his distress.

'I'm Gina,' she said at last, placing herself where he could see her. 'What's your name?'

She already knew that he was called Joey, but she wanted him to tell her himself. That would start them communicating.

He looked at her, then away. After a moment he looked back.

'Don't you want to tell me?'

He took a deep breath and made a noise that sounded like, 'Oooeeey!'

'Joey? That's fine. My name is Gina.' He frowned, so she said it again. He tried, not very successfully, to say the word.

'Look,' she said, holding up her hand.

Slowly she made the sign for G, then I. She wondered if he understood finger-spelling, but his eyes brightened, and she finished the word.

'Gina,' she said.

He tried to say it. It came out badly but she smiled encouragement, and spelt it again with her fingers. Joey watched intently, then repeated her movements exactly.

'Well done,' she said, spelling the two words.

He tried to follow her and got it right on the second try.

'Have something to eat now, and we'll try again later,' she said.

Now that he'd calmed down, she could study him better, and she saw sadness, as if the weight of the world was crushing him.

She ventured to try a longer sentence. 'Are you enjoying your biscuits?'

He nodded, tried to say something and choked on a crumb. She patted him on the back and they laughed together.

Then it was his turn. He tried to speak some words which Gina almost understood. Some signalling back and forth revealed the meaning: *You must eat biscuits, too.*

After that the conversation was fast and furious. A light came into the child's face. He communicated as if he'd never managed it before.

'I'm deaf, too,' she told him. 'I can hear now, but I know what it's like. Nobody understands.'

He nodded and, eyes wide, repeated with his fingers, *Nobody understands.*

'You're very clever,' Gina told him, her fingers working fast.

Joey simply stared. Gina said it again and indicated for him to spell the words too. But instead of doing so he made a single sound.

'Eeee?' he said.

Something stuck in Gina's throat. Instinctively she knew the meaning of that pathetic question.

'Yes, darling, you,' she said. 'You're very clever. You really are.'

This time he didn't try to answer, but simply shook his head forlornly. Gina couldn't bear that sight. She put her arms about him and hugged him to her. He hugged her back, clutching her so fiercely that she gasped.

I'm a stranger, she thought. Yet the poor little soul clings to me.

She closed her eyes and held on to him tightly, trying to convey comfort and safety in a way he could understand. When she opened her eyes again, Carson Page was standing in the doorway, watching them with an expression from which all emotion had been carefully wiped.

'It's time for us to go,' he said.

Reluctantly Gina tried to release herself from the little boy's arms, but Joey tightened his grip and wailed.

'All right,' she said quickly. She turned his face to her and said slowly, 'Don't worry. I'm here.'

She didn't know what had made her say that in defiance of his father, but at that moment she would have done anything for this little boy.

'I'm taking him home,' Carson said firmly.

Gina faced Joey. 'Home,' she said.

But the child shook his head wildly. And when his father took hold of him, he began to thrash about, trying to fight him off.

'Come along,' Carson said firmly, tightening his grip.

'Let him go!' Gina rose to face him.

'What did you say?'

'I said, let him go. You've no right to treat him like this.'

'Are you out of your mind?'

'I'm asking you to be gentle with him—'

'I make every effort to do so, but I will not tolerate tantrums.'

At the word 'tantrums', Gina wanted to bang her head against the wall—or preferably bang his head against the wall. Was there any way of getting through to this man?

'He's not having a tantrum,' she said through gritted teeth. 'He's lonely and frightened. *Are you such a monster that you can't tell the difference?*'

Carson stared at her, thunderstruck by the force of her attack. She was amazed at it herself. Her nature was normally placid, but Joey's suffering had brought old fears and miseries to the surface, destroying her control. For a moment she was a child again, lashing out at a cruel world that didn't care enough to understand.

Then she saw Philip Hale in the doorway and her heart sank.

'You will collect your things, Miss Tennison, and leave immediately,' Mr Hale said, in a voice that contained a hint of triumph.

'No,' Carson said at once. 'I owe Miss Tennison a debt, and I can't allow her to lose her job.'

Philip Hale's face was a picture. The desire not to

offend a valuable client warred with indignation at
Carson's imperious way of declaring what he would and
wouldn't allow. While he was struggling Carson went
on without waiting for a reply.

'Miss Tennison, I thank you for saving my son,
and—' for the first time he seemed to falter '—and for
the understanding you have shown him. You're a credit
to your employers, and I shall be writing to the senior
partners to say so.' He emphasised 'senior' very slightly.
Philip Hale noticed and his eyes narrowed.

Gina let out a slow breath, more confused than she'd
ever been. He was brusque, harsh and arrogant, but he
was also fair.

Carson reached out to Joey. All the fight seemed to
have drained out of the child, and he took his father's
hand without protest. But he was weeping with a kind
of resigned despair that broke Gina's heart.

She watched as father and son walked out and headed
for the front door. They got halfway. Then Carson
stopped and looked down at the child who, by now, was
wiping his face. He put his fingers under the boy's chin,
and lifted it, looking urgently into his eyes. Then, more
gently than Gina would have believed possible, he took
out a handkerchief and dried the little boy's tears. He
looked back at her. For the first time he seemed unsure
of himself.

'You'd better come with us,' he said. 'I mean—if you
can spare the time.'

Gina opened her mouth to say that of course she
would come, but suddenly she was swept by alarm. She
wanted to help this vulnerable child, yet a great weight
seemed to be crushing her.

'I—I—' she stammered.

'Go with him and make yourself useful,' Hale said,

speaking through gritted teeth. 'I shall have things to say to you later.'

She collected her bag and hurried to catch up with them. Joey watched her, eyes wide, smiling. Then he put up his hands and spelled out, 'Come too.'

'Yes,' she said, clearly. 'I'm coming, too.'

'Then let's go,' Carson said.

CHAPTER THREE

ON THE journey, nobody spoke. Sitting in the rear, with Joey, Gina could only see the back of Carson's head. It had a forbidding look. The child seemed simply content to have her there. Gina was trying to calm herself, battling with traumas she had thought would never trouble her again.

For a while she'd been back in the old nightmare of childhood, hemmed in by silence and misunderstanding. It was a prison from which she'd hoped she'd escaped, but suddenly the walls had been there again. Now she was struggling with herself. She didn't want to return to that prison, and yet Joey's need was so great...

What was she thinking of? she wondered. This was one brief visit, and then she would never see either Joey or his father again.

She was bitterly disillusioned by Carson. Was it only yesterday that she'd thought she detected charm and kindness beneath his gruff manners? Goodness, had she been wrong about that!

The truth about him was that he was as prejudiced about deafness as anyone else, and furious at the fate that had given him a deaf child. To blazes with him! she thought stormily.

She realised that the little boy was trying to catch her attention, spelling out some words. She answered with her fingers, and they chatted in silence for the rest of the journey.

She soon recognised the part of London where they

were heading. It was a place where rich men chose to live to show their status, with broad, tree-lined streets and large detached dwellings standing well back from the road. She'd once arranged the purchase of a house like one of these, and knew that they cost a million.

At last they slowed outside the largest mansion in the street, and Carson turned into the sweeping, curved drive and past the trees that hid the house from passers-by.

'Normally Mrs Saunders would be here,' he explained as he opened the front door. 'She runs everything and looks after Joey when he's not at school, but at the last moment she needed the day off, which is why I had to take him with me.'

'Yes, I could tell you weren't very experienced in looking after him,' Gina said wryly.

They had stepped into a large hall with polished wooden floors and a broad staircase. The house was pleasant, with tall windows, and through the open doors she could see sunlit rooms. It might have been a lovely place to live, but to Gina's eyes there was something unwelcoming about it. It was spotless, and everything was of the best. But it wasn't a home to the two people who lived here, each trapped in his own isolation.

She was beginning to be worried by the looks Joey gave her, and the way he held her hand, as though she was vital to him. She mustn't be. She could only do her best for him and pass on.

Yet she couldn't help remembering the way people had come and gone in her own childhood, the feeling that here was someone who understood, only to find them vanished in a week.

Joey was pulling her hand, urging her out towards the garden. She followed him, with Carson bringing up the rear. It was a large, beautiful place, with magnificent lawns and flowerbeds. But Joey had no time for their beauties. He almost dragged Gina to a large pond where fat fish idled around. He pointed each out in turn, and chatted about them with his fingers.

'He's very interested in fish,' Carson said, catching up with them. There was an undertone of desperation in his voice, as though he was making conscientious efforts, but wasn't sure what came next.

Gina noted the effort, but still blamed him. Joey had been his son for several years, and he ought to be able to cope better than this.

Joey left them for a moment to go around to the far side of the pool and study the water. He was frowning and his concentration was so intense that he looked like a little professor.

'Why doesn't Philip Hale like you?' Carson asked suddenly. 'It's more than you told me yesterday, isn't it?'

'Yes. He considers me "disabled" and he can't handle that. Some people can't cope with anyone out of the ordinary.' She regarded him levelly.

'Was that meant for me?' he demanded.

'Would it be true?'

'You evidently think so. You don't like people who make snap judgements, do you? But today you judged me and found me wanting very quickly. No mitigating circumstances, no "let's learn all the facts". Just "off with his head".'

There was just enough truth in that to make her uncomfortable.

'Carson, please don't think I'm not grateful to you for saving my job. It was decent of you, after the things I said to you.'

'A simple matter of justice,' he said coolly. 'Besides, you can be useful to me.'

'Yes, I thought it might be something like that.'

'You don't take any prisoners, do you?' he said wryly.

'Well, if there's a battle, I'm on Joey's side. I fought it years ago. Don't be fooled by my appearance. I may look like a little brown mouse, but I'm really very tough.'

'Little brown mouse?' he echoed. 'With that blazing auburn hair?'

She was taken aback. She was used to thinking of her hair as sandy, or at most 'reddish'; certainly at the dull end of the red spectrum. Nobody had ever suggested before that it was at the glamorous end.

All the way back to the house Joey watched the two of them closely, aware of their tension. Once inside he began to pull on Gina's hand, urging her to the stairs.

'Please, go with him,' Carson said.

She wasn't sure what to expect from Joey's room, but the reality made her stop and stare. It wasn't that the walls were covered with posters—it was the content of the posters that astonished her. Not a footballer in sight.

Everywhere she looked there were whales, penguins, sharks, sea lions, fish, coral, shells. The bookshelves took up the same theme, and beyond them were more shelves of videos.

'You must know a great deal,' Gina told Joey.

He nodded.

'Have you always been interested in marine life?'

She had to spell marine, but then he understood and nodded again.

He showed her around, and she found that he had all that money could buy, including a computer through which he could pursue his interest on the Internet. His father had even provided a credit card with which he could purchase whatever he pleased from an on-line bookshop.

In fact, the room had everything except some sign of warm, adult interest. This child lived in a vacuum, Gina thought with a shiver. On the evidence of his books he was highly intelligent, but he had nobody to share it with.

And then she found something that struck a curious note. A large framed photograph stood by Joey's bed. It showed a young woman in her early twenties. Her face was heavily made up, but even without that she would have been beautiful. Her rich blonde hair tumbled over her shoulders and her mouth was curved provocatively at the camera.

Gina recognised the woman. She was a young actress called Angelica Duvaine who was fast making a name for herself in films. Gina had seen her playing second lead in a recent blockbuster. She had a limited talent but her beauty and glamour were stunning. It was a strange picture to find in the room of such a young child.

Joey saw her looking and beamed with pride.

'My mother,' he spelled.

'But—' Gina realised she was entering a minefield. A child, cruelly deprived of his own mother, had set up this fantasy to comfort himself. How could she snatch it from him?

'She's very pretty,' Gina agreed.

Joey nodded and pointed to the picture. 'Eeee—aye— eeee,' he said.

Gina understood this as *She gave me*. A fan picture, sent through the post, and the child thought he'd been selected for special favour.

'She gave it to you?' she echoed. 'That was nice of her.'

Joey fought for speech. The result was garbled but Gina understood. *She loves me.*

'Yes,' she said heavily. 'Of course she does.'

Carson looked in. 'There's something to eat downstairs.'

Supper was laid in the elegant dining room, full of polished rosewood, with expensive pictures on the wall. Gina reflected that she would have hated to be a child in such a room, and Joey seemed to feel the same, because he was subdued.

The meal was excellent, and she complimented Carson on it.

'I can't take the credit,' he admitted. 'Mrs Saunders left everything ready and I just microwaved it.' He regarded his son, staring unenthusiastically at his plate. 'What?' He touched Joey's shoulder to get his attention. 'What's the matter with it?' he asked, raising his voice.

'Does Joey have any hearing at all?' Gina asked.

'No, none.'

'Then why do you shout? Speaking clearly is what he needs, so that he can follow your lips. Anyway, there's nothing the matter with the food. But if Joey's like me at that age he'd prefer a burger.'

'Junk food,' Carson said disparagingly. 'This is better for him.'

She saw Joey looking from one to the other with the bewildered look of the excluded, and took his hand in hers for a moment. At once the look of strain vanished from his face.

'But who wants to have what's better for them all the time?' she persisted. 'Junk is more fun. Have you ever asked him what he prefers?'

'That isn't easy.'

'Yes, it is,' she insisted. 'You look into his face so that he can see your lips.'

'Do you think I don't try that? He doesn't understand me. Or he chooses not to, for reasons of his own.'

Gina was about to dispute this but a memory of her childhood got in the way.

'That depends how you talk to him,' she mused. 'If you let him see you're impatient, he's bound to get upset.'

'I do not—well, I try not to—are you saying he is doing it deliberately?'

'I don't know, but it's what I used to do. When you're faced with a really unsympathetic adult who's obviously just doing his duty, and would rather be anywhere but with you—you don't tend to make it easy for him.'

'And I am the unsympathetic adult, I take it?'

'Are you?'

He let out a long, slow breath. 'I'm doing my best.'

'How good a best is it?'

'It's damnable,' he flashed. 'All right? That's what you think, isn't it? And it's the truth. I'm a lousy father, I don't know what I'm doing and he's suffering for it.'

'At least you're honest.'

'But where does honesty get us?' he asked bleakly. 'Do you have the answer any more than I do?'

The weight of despair in his voice checked her condemnation. He too was suffering, and he coped less well than the child.

Last night, the word 'deaf' had made a change come over him and she'd judged him severely, assuming that he'd reacted with repulsion, as so many people did. But the truth was that deafness confronted him with problems he couldn't cope with, and a miserable awareness of his own failure.

'What should I do?' he said wearily. 'For God's sake, tell me if you know!'

'I can tell you what it's like for Joey,' she said. 'If you understood that, you might find things easier for both of you.' She saw Joey looking at them and said, 'Not now,' quietly to Carson.

For the rest of the meal she concentrated on the child, making him feel included. Carson ate very little, but he watched them, his eyes moving from one to the other as though he was afraid to miss anything.

'May I use your telephone?' Gina asked after a while. She'd remembered that Dan was due to call her.

'There's one in that room through there,' Carson said.

She called Dan's mobile and found him slightly tetchy.

'You didn't say you were going to be out tonight,' he complained.

'I didn't know. Something came up suddenly.'

'My boss invited me to his house and said to bring you, too. It didn't look good when I turned up without you.'

'I'm sorry, but I didn't know.'

'You've still got time to get here if you hurry.'

'All right, I'll try to—'

Then she saw Joey watching her from the doorway.

His face told her that he understood. He couldn't hear the words, but when you were deaf you always knew when people were preparing to desert you.

Desert? Nonsense! She didn't owe Joey anything.

But she did. Because he was trapped in the dreadful silent world from which she had escaped. And the deaf always owed each other, because they knew terrible secrets that nobody else knew.

'I'm sorry, I can't,' she said hurriedly.

'Gina, this is important.'

'And my job is important to me,' she said, seizing an excuse that Dan would understand. 'I blotted my copybook with a client this afternoon, and I'm trying to put it right.' Hurriedly she explained about the accident, and about Joey. She could sense Dan becoming interested.

'Carson Page? The man you were talking to last night?'

'Yes.'

'You're at his home?'

'Yes.'

'That posh place in Belmere Avenue?'

'Yes.'

'Hmm. All right. I'll be in touch.'

He hung up.

Carson had come to the door to urge Joey back to the table. It was clear he'd heard part of the conversation. He looked at her wryly.

'Did I force you to break a date?' he asked.

'No, there's no problem.' She spoke to Joey. 'I'm not going yet.'

His brilliant smile was her reward.

After the meal Joey, at a nod from his father, switched on the television to watch his favourite soap, with the aid of subtitles. The two of them cleared the plates into the kitchen. Carson poured her a glass of wine, and pulled out a chair at the table.

'I haven't told you properly how grateful I am,' he said. 'I should never have taken Joey to that place, but I didn't know what else to do. He broke up from school today and, without Mrs Saunders, I had to take him with me. I got absorbed in business and didn't see him wander off. But for you, I might have lost him.' He added quietly. 'And I couldn't bear that. He's all I have.'

'I wish you'd asked me to look after him at the office this afternoon,' Gina said.

'I thought of it, but I didn't know how, without breaking my word and admitting that we'd met before.'

'You should have broken it,' she said at once.

'Also, I wasn't sure if your employers knew about you. I didn't want to let the cat out of the bag, precisely because there are people like Philip Hale in the world.'

'I thought you were like him,' she admitted. 'Last night—'

'I didn't react very well, I know. But it's like floundering in a sea of confusion. I try to remind myself that it's worse for Joey.'

'Yes, poor little soul. Outsiders can't imagine—the sheer frustration when the words are building up inside you and you can't get them out—and people look at you as if you're crazy—'

'If that's meant for me, don't bother. We've already agreed that I'm a hopeless father with no idea what his son needs.'

'Surely you know one thing that he needs? His mother. Even if you and she have fallen out, she's the person with the best chance of understanding him. If he had her, he wouldn't have to indulge in fairy tales about film stars.'

'What makes you think he's indulging in fairy tales?' Carson asked wryly.

'Oh, please! I've seen Angelica Duvaine's picture by his bed. She looks about twenty.'

'She'd be thrilled to hear you say so. She's twenty-eight. That picture's been cleverly touched up. Mind you, even the reality looks much younger than the fact. She's worked on her appearance—diet, massage, exercise. The next thing was going to be plastic surgery to lift her breasts. It was the row over that that made her finally move out. Not that she was here much anyway, by that time.'

'Are you telling me that Angelica Duvaine really is Joey's mother?' Gina asked, only half believing.

'In a sense. Her real name is Brenda Page but it's years since she answered to it. When our divorce is finalised in a few weeks she won't even be that any more.

'I know I look like the monster separating mother and child, but I wouldn't be doing it if she showed any interest in him. You should read some of Brenda's press interviews. She's never once told the world she has a son. From the moment she realised Joey had a problem with his hearing, he ceased to exist as far as she was concerned. He was a blot, something to be ashamed of. My wife, you see, values physical perfection above everything.'

He waited a moment, to see if she had any answer for this.

'Oh, dear God!' Gina whispered at last. 'That poor little boy.'

'Joey adores her. God knows why, when she treats him so carelessly. She goes away, ignores him, comes back for five minutes, then goes away and breaks his heart again. But he never holds it against her, no matter how badly she behaves.'

'Of course not,' Gina said. 'He thinks it's his fault.'

He looked at her strangely. 'Is that how it was for you?'

'Something like that. I was lucky in my mother—she was wonderful, but she died. My father—well, I think he actually found me repellent. And I knew I must have done something terrible to make him not love me.'

'And that's what Joey thinks?'

'He told me that his mother loves him. He probably explains her absences by blaming himself. But I'm only guessing.'

'So what do I do?' Carson demanded. 'Explain to him that his mother is a selfish woman who loves nobody but herself? That she remembers him when it suits her and abandons him when it suits her? Why do you think I'm trying to separate them finally? Because I can't stand the look on his face when she leaves again—as she always does.'

'But she's his mother—she must love him, in her own way—'

'Then why didn't she take him with her? I wouldn't have tried to stop her, if she'd really wanted him. Don't judge every mother by your own. They're not all wonderful.'

'I'm sorry,' she said helplessly. 'I had no right to criticise you without knowing all the facts.'

He ran a hand through his hair, dishevelling it. At some point he'd removed his tie and torn open the throat of his shirt. The man in control had slipped away, leaving only the man distracted by forces he didn't understand.

'I guess I can't blame you on that score,' he said. 'It's something I do myself. What are all the facts? How can you ever know?'

'Tell me about Mrs Saunders. Is she qualified to help Joey?'

'I thought so. Brenda hired her. Apparently she once worked in a school for children with special needs. But

Joey dislikes her. He has violent tantrums. Only yesterday he had a terrible screaming fit.'

'But that's frustration. It's not fair to call it a tantrum.'

'Maybe not. But I think that's why Mrs Saunders took today off. She needed a rest. Who's that?'

The doorbell had rung. Frowning, Carson went to answer it, and returned with Dan.

'You said your car was still being repaired,' he explained, 'so I thought I'd give you a lift home.'

'Very thoughtful,' Carson said, 'but I would have provided Miss Tennison with a taxi.' He looked at her reluctantly. 'Were you anxious to leave?'

'That depends on Joey.'

'It's about his bedtime.'

'Why don't you put him to bed?' Dan said to Gina. 'I'm sure he'd like that.'

His smile was full of cheerful kindness, yet it struck a strangely false note with Gina. She didn't have time to brood over it. She signed *bedtime* to Joey, and he jumped up and came with her eagerly.

'I won't be long,' she told the two men.

'Don't hurry too much, darling,' Dan muttered to her. 'I've been trying to meet Carson Page for months.'

So that was it. She couldn't really blame Dan. He worked hard and he had his way to make in the world. But tonight had been about Joey and his needs, and Dan's opportunism jarred with her.

While Joey got into the shower she returned to his room to fetch the towelling robe she'd seen hanging behind his door. On the way back, she stopped and looked over the banisters. She could just see where Dan and Carson were sitting together, talking. At least, Dan was talking. All she could see of Carson was his back, but something in the set of his shoulders told her that he was finding Dan's monologue hard going.

Joey turned off the shower and came out straight into the bathrobe she was holding up for him.

'An—ooo!' he said painfully. *Thank you.*

She put him to bed, and asked him, signing, if he wanted to read. He shook his head and lay looking up at her from his pillow, smiling. He seemed relaxed and happy, quite different from the tense, nervous child of the afternoon. Impulsively Gina leaned down and kissed him.

'Is he ready to go to sleep?' Carson asked from the door.

'Just waiting for you to come and say goodnight,' Gina told him.

She stood back so that father and son could hug each other, but Carson only said awkwardly, 'Goodnight, son.'

Joey struggled to say goodnight, and managed the word pretty well, but Gina could feel Carson's tension.

'Goodnight, Joey,' she said.

She was about to turn away, but Joey detained her with a hand on her arm. She sat on his bed and watched as he pointed at himself, then curled over the middle three fingers of his hand so that the thumb and the little finger made a Y shape. With this he made a gentle waving motion, then finished by pointing at her. A shy smile touched his lips.

'What did he say?' Carson asked.

'He says he likes me.' Smiling, Gina indicated herself, made the Y gesture, then pointed at Joey.

I like you.

Suddenly she was gasping for breath as a pair of young arms tightened around her neck in an embrace that was both eager and desperate. She hugged him back, but it was some time before she could make him release her.

She felt torn in two. She wanted to stay and do everything she could for Joey. But she also wanted to flee this house that reminded her of so much pain.

At last he let go, and lay down quietly, but his shining eyes followed her until she closed the door.

'Thank you,' Carson said. 'That meant the world to him. When will you come back?'

'Is it really a good idea for me to come back?'

'I don't understand. You lecture me about Joey's needs, but you can help him better than I can.'

'But I'm not his father—or his mother. It's you that's got to get onto his wavelength. Put him first and take your cue from that.'

'All right,' he said after a moment.

Downstairs, Dan looked as though he'd like to settle in for a long talk, but Carson adroitly prevented this, apologising for keeping her so late. Reluctantly Dan rose to go.

'Goodnight, Miss Tennison,' Carson said formally. 'I'll think over what you've said.'

In the car Dan was euphoric. 'If I can sell our spark plugs to Page Engineering it'll be a feather in my cap. I thought I'd never get to meet him.'

'I'm sorry if I let you down, but how could I refuse when that little boy—'

'I told him all about our plugs and he seemed really interested. He wants me to call at his office, and take him the full details, and I just knew—it's a feeling you get when you know you're going down really well, and the customer is hanging on every word.'

'I'm very glad for you, Dan.'

'Well, I owe part of it to you,' he said generously. 'Well done, darling. You know, that's one of the best things about you. You're always so reliable.'

'Thank you,' she said. 'It's nice to know.'

It was a compliment, of a sort. But then she found herself recalling Carson saying, 'Little brown mouse? With that blazing auburn hair?'

But he hadn't meant to compliment her at all.

She refused Dan's offer of a drink. She felt suddenly very tired after the emotions of the day. He dropped her at her flat and drove away, his head full of spark plugs and deals to be done.

Before going to bed that night Gina looked at herself in the mirror. Slowly she pulled her hair about her face and studied it for a long time. At last she drew a long breath of pure disbelieving pleasure.

It *was* blazing auburn.

And she had never noticed before.

CHAPTER FOUR

'THE position is really a little difficult,' George Wainright said. 'It's a pity Philip has taken agin you.'

They were sitting in George's office next morning. As Gina had feared, he'd already received an account of yesterday's incident, embellished with Philip's dislike.

'Luckily, Mr Page has written a letter praising you in glowing terms,' George went on. 'It was hand-delivered first thing this morning, and it will certainly help. But we can't have you losing your temper with the customers.'

George Wainright was an elderly man who looked like everyone's favourite grandad, but Gina wasn't fooled. He was tough, and right now his manner was implacable.

'Anyway, let's leave it there for the moment,' he said. 'Go on doing an excellent job, and it'll soon die down.'

As the day wore on Gina began to hope that everything really would be all right. Meeting Joey had shaken her up, but with time, and calm, she would get herself in hand.

Then, halfway through the afternoon, she received a call from the receptionist to say she had a visitor. And something in her tone told Gina who the visitor was.

With a sinking heart she went out to the front desk. There was Joey, looking anxious but determined.

She whisked him into her office, and closed the door on prying eyes. Speaking and signing together, she asked, 'What are you doing here?'

He answered with his fingers. *I wanted to see you.*

'Did anybody come with you?'

No. I just wanted you.

'Has something happened?'

Instead of answering directly he shrugged and looked at the floor. Gina's alarm grew. Something had upset the boy, but this wasn't the time to badger him with questions. She called Page Engineering.

A barrage of assistants and secretaries barred her access to Carson Page, until she said firmly, 'Tell him it's Miss Tennison, about his son,' and this worked like magic.

Carson's voice came as a shock. She had forgotten that it was so deep and attractive.

'Mr Page, I have Joey here. He found his way to my office alone and he's upset about something.'

'Alone? Where's Mrs Saunders?'

'Wait, I'll ask him.'

She spelled out the name carefully, and Joey made a sign that surprised her so much that she made him repeat it.

'Carson, he says she's gone away.'

'And left him alone in the house?'

More signing. 'He says yes.'

Carson swore.

'Can you come and collect him?' she asked. 'He's upset and he needs to be reassured.'

'I'm in an urgent meeting. Besides, I'm not the one he wants. It's you he came to, not me.'

'But you're his father. Put him first, for heaven's sake.'

'Give me five minutes; I'll call you back,' he said brusquely.

As she hung up she saw Joey looking at her. He knew

she'd been speaking to his father, and it was there in his face that he also knew what the answer was. His expression wasn't sad. Rather, it asked her what else she had expected, and it was a terrible look for a child to wear.

She gave him something to eat and they chatted. Gina gathered that Mrs Saunders had gone out late that morning, saying she would return 'soon', but after three hours there was no sign of her.

Abandoned in his silence, he had headed for the one person who made him feel safe—not his father, but Gina.

'How did you get here?' she asked.

I wrote your address on a piece of paper. Then I walked to the railway station. There's a taxi rank.

Eight, vulnerable, abandoned. Walking the streets alone.

At last Carson called back.

'I'm afraid I'll have to trespass on your kindness a little more,' he said. 'Will you take Joey home for me, please, and stay until I can get there? I've cleared it with your boss. Have you got your car back yet?'

'Yes. But how do I get into your house?'

'There's a spare key under the rose bush by the porch. Joey knows where it is. I'll be there as quickly as I can. Thank you for doing this for me.'

'You haven't given me much ch—' But he'd hung up.

George Wainright appeared in her door, beaming.

'Well, that's all right, then,' he said genially. 'Philip and I have agreed that the best thing is to release you for as long as you need.'

'You mean, Carson Page has agreed that I should be released for as long as he needs,' Gina said wryly.

'Well, it was a bit like that, I must admit,' George

admitted. 'But if you keep him sweet the whole firm benefits.'

Gina was left with no choice but to leave with Joey. As before, in her company his tensions fell away and he became quietly happy.

They went out to the car park and found the 'peanut', at which point Joey's eyes widened and he became sorely tried, his natural good manners struggling with his mirth.

'Et tu, Brute?' she murmured.

What was that? he signed.

'It means that everyone laughs at my poor little car— even you.'

Manners lost the battle. *But it's funny.*

'Oh, all right. I'll tell you how I met your father the other day.'

She described the incident, including how she'd had to climb into the car from the back, and he collapsed with amusement.

'You do it,' she said, opening the boot, and he scrambled through in delight.

They reached the house to find only silence. There was no sign of Mrs Saunders, but the phone started ringing as they entered. It was the local hospital.

'Mrs Saunders asked us to call this number and leave a message on the answeing machine,' said a female voice. 'She was involved in a motor accident—knocked down by a car. She isn't seriously hurt, but she'll be in here for a few days.'

So that mystery, at least, was explained. She told Joey what had happened, emphasising that Mrs Saunders hadn't deserted him deliberately. But he seemed more concerned with the fact that now he would have Gina to himself. His delight was touching, even though it dismayed her.

'Right,' she told him. 'Let's make this an adventure.'

For dinner, she found eggs and bacon, plus some ice cream in the freezer, and the two of them had a banquet. Between mouthfuls they talked in silence. Joey chattered and chattered, as though something had suddenly set him free.

She understood. There were people who talked with you as a duty and people who seemed to enjoy talking with you. And when you found one of the latter you made the most of them.

Gradually the shape of Joey's personality was becoming clear to her. He was lively, brave and intelligent, with a neat sense of humour. And when he got onto his favourite subject, marine life, he was unstoppable. This was more than a child's interest, Gina realised. He really knew his stuff.

As they were putting the dishes away, the phone rang. Probably Carson, to say he was going to be late.

But the voice on the other end was female, and throatily seductive. 'I don't believe I know you.'

'My name's Gina Tennison and I'm here to look after Joey.'

'Well, I'm Angelica Duvaine. Please fetch Carson.'

'I'm afraid he isn't here. He was kept late at a meeting.'

'Oh, I can believe that. Him and his meetings! No time for his wife but always time for those damned meetings.'

'But Joey is here. He'll be thrilled that you called. I'll fetch him.'

'Whatever for? I mean, he can't hear me, can he?'

Gina drew a long breath. The impatience and irritation in the other woman's voice had been too clear to miss.

'No, but I can do sign language and interpret for you,' she said.

'Look, can you just give Carson a message?'

'I'll take your message when you've spoken to Joey,' Gina said firmly. 'I'll fetch him now.'

She heard a sharp gasp from the other end. This woman wasn't used to being defied. Gina beckoned Joey to the phone and signed, *Mother*. Instantly the child's face was brilliant with joy. He seized the receiver, and made a sound into it that Gina interpreted as, 'Hello, Mummy.'

Gina took the receiver. 'What shall I tell him from you?' she asked.

'Well—say hello—and I hope he's being a good boy.'

'Shall I tell him that you love him?' Gina asked, concealing her anger for Joey's sake.

'Yes—yes, tell him that.'

Gina signed. *Mummy says she hopes you're being a good boy and she loves you very much.*

'Joey says, where are you?'

'I'm in Los Angeles.'

'He wants to know if you miss him.'

'Of course I miss him. He's my darling little son.'

Gina signed this accurately, and Joey beamed.

It was hard but she kept some sort of conversation going, prompting Angelica when she was stuck. Once she knew what was expected of her, Angelica got into the role, managing to say more or less the right things. And occasionally Gina embellished, to make the other woman's faltering remarks sound better. Joey was in seventh heaven.

Then the front door opened and Carson came in.

He nodded a greeting to Gina, and headed for the kitchen.

'Wait,' Gina called to him. 'It's your ex-wife on the line. Just a moment.' She turned back to the receiver. 'Joey says—'

Carson seemed to become aware of what was happening. A slight frown creased his forehead as Gina relayed Angelica's words, suitably edited, back to the child.

'Mummy has to go now, but she says she loves you— Joey says he loves you too, very much, and he wants to know when—'

She broke off as Carson snatched the phone from her. 'Brenda, what the hell are you playing at?'

Gina shepherded Joey away. Luckily he was too happy to be troubled by his father's abrupt action. She tried not to eavesdrop but Carson didn't bother to lower his voice.

'I told you to deal through my lawyer—and don't give me that yearning mother act, because I'm not fooled any more. I was fooled for years—about that and a few other things—but not now.'

He hung up sharply and swung around to Gina. 'I ought to ask what the hell *you* imagine you're playing at,' he said furiously. 'Do you think I can't see through that little farce? Brenda, sending loving messages to her son! I'll bet she was never so surprised in her life.'

'But it meant the world to him—'

'Got his hopes up, you mean. How will he feel when she doesn't follow through? Did you stop to think of that?'

'No,' she admitted, dismayed. 'I just wanted to give him a little happiness. I didn't think about afterwards. I'm sorry.'

'Of all the stupid—!'

Then he realised his son was watching him.

'Hello, son.' Joey couldn't hear the words, but he saw his father's hand outstretched to him. Carson's manner was awkward, but there was affection in the way he ruffled the boy's hair. And when Joey's arms went around him Carson returned the embrace fiercely. Gina caught a glimpse of his face before he bent it over Joey's head, and she looked quickly away.

She hadn't been meant to see the mixture of unhappiness and helpless love in Carson's face. That was for his child, if he could find the way to show it.

'We've eaten,' she said, following him into the kitchen. 'But I'll make you something.'

'What's happened to Mrs Saunders?'

'She's in hospital. She went out—to do some shopping, I suppose—and was knocked down in the street. It's not serious, but she'll be there for a few days.'

'A few days?' he echoed, aghast. 'Damn! I'm sorry she's hurt, of course, but she had no right to leave Joey alone here, even for a moment.'

'I agree. But he managed brilliantly. He remembered my address from the other day, wrote it down and found himself a taxi. He's a really bright child.'

'Yes, he knew exactly who to head for, didn't he?' he asked heavily.

To her astonishment, she realised that he was hurt. He hadn't wanted his meeting interrupted, but it hurt him that Joey hadn't even tried.

'He knows how busy you are—' she began.

He flung her a look. 'Don't rub it in. Just tell me what's going to happen now—without Mrs Saunders.'

'Well, obviously I'm going to be here until she returns,' Gina said lightly. 'I thought you'd have decided that already.'

'I—was going to *ask* you if you'd consider taking us on for a while,' Carson said, picking his words carefully. 'You seem to be able to cope with anything.'

She smiled. 'I guess I can cope with you and Joey.'

'What, both of us?' he asked, rallying his defences.

'Both of you. Joey's the easy one.'

'Thank you,' he said with a touch of ruefulness. 'I don't know how I'd manage if you weren't here.'

She scribbled a number on a piece of paper, and gave it to him.

'That's George Wainright's home number. You can settle it with him while I put Joey to bed.'

He regarded her askance. 'Think you've got me sized up, don't you?'

'Well, it's not difficult,' she said indignantly. 'I just take it for granted that your juggernaut will ride on over us all, and I get it right every time.'

'And you think that's all I am? A juggernaut?'

No, she thought, remembering the first day. There was something else in him, something that had seen the funny side of their collision and behaved generously, tried awkwardly to reach out to her, and then drawn back hastily. Something she wanted to know more about.

'I think you're a juggernaut when it suits you,' she said.

'And you think it suits me a lot, don't you?'

'Since you're virtually my employer now, it wouldn't be proper for me to answer that question.'

'And do you always do what's proper?'

'You know I don't. That's why I'm in trouble at work—because I told you off.'

Suddenly his attractive smile broke out. 'Say what you like. I won't tell on you.'

She couldn't help answering the smile. 'I'm going to put Joey to bed. Why don't you make that phone call?'

'Whatever you say.'

She came down half an hour later, having seen Joey nod off contentedly. Carson was waiting for her. 'Can we talk?'

'I'm afraid it'll have to be later. If I'm going to stay here I've got to dash home and get some clothes.'

'Will you be long?'

'I'll try not to be. A couple of hours, maybe.'

'I'll drive you—no, I can't leave Joey alone, can I? It's a pity he's already in bed—'

'Carson,' she said gently, 'sooner or later you're going to have to learn to be alone with him.'

'Yes.' He grimaced. 'I don't come out of this very well, do I?'

'You're trying to do your best.'

'My best seems to consist of clinging onto you. I guess he's not the only one holding your hand.'

'Well, I have a very steady hand,' she assured him. 'I'll be back as soon as I can.'

Her little flat was a world away from Carson's luxurious mansion, but it was her own, and when she'd hastily packed a suitcase she gave a regretful glance around.

'Just a couple of days,' she assured herself. 'Then I'll be back.'

The streets were clear and she managed the journey fairly quickly. Even so, she arrived to find him standing in the porch, watching for her anxiously.

'Joey awoke and found you gone,' he said. 'He

thought you'd abandoned him. I tried to reassure him, but I—I can't reach him.'

From behind him Gina could hear moaning. She hurried past and saw Joey sitting on the stairs, his arms wrapped around his knees, rocking back and forth in misery. Tears poured down his face, and at first even she couldn't get through to him.

She took hold of his shoulders, and at last she managed to get him looking at her.

'I'm here,' she said clearly. 'Joey, I'm here. I haven't gone away.'

He began to sign but he was too overwrought to organise himself and the attempt collapsed. He tried to speak. Gina listened carefully while he repeated the words again and again.

'What's he saying?' Carson asked desperately.

'He says he awoke and I wasn't there,' Gina interpreted at last.

'But I was,' Carson shouted.

She signed. *Daddy was here.*

Joey shook his head violently, pointing at Gina.

'Don't tell me,' Carson said heavily. 'I guess I understood that.'

'I'll take him back to bed.'

It took time to calm Joey down, but at last he was ready to attend quietly while she explained where she'd been. When he heard that she'd collected clothes for a stay he brightened.

Stay, he signed happily.

'Just for a few days.'

Stay.

She sighed and left it there. This wasn't the time to tell him that she would leave when Mrs Saunders returned. Let him be happy while he could. She waited until he was asleep, kissed him, and crept out of the room.

Carson was waiting outside. 'I've put you in this room next to Joey,' he said. 'It's a bit small but it has a connecting door to him.'

'That's ideal.'

The bed was stripped, but Carson showed her the airing cupboard, found sheets and blankets for her, and, to her surprise, even helped her make up the bed.

'You have a talent for this,' she said, observing his neat corners.

'My mother made sure I did, or it was a clip round the ear. She taught me how to make coffee, too. I'll have some ready downstairs, when you're finished in here.'

She went down a few minutes later to find him in the living room, with freshly perked coffee on a low table.

'Is he all right?' he asked.

'Yes, fast asleep.'

'Now that *you're* here.'

She settled down and gratefully took the coffee he handed her. He watched her quizzically while she sipped it.

'Perfect,' she said.

'I told you, I've been well trained.'

An uneasy silence fell between them.

'I've always prided myself on being on top of every situation,' he said at last. 'In business, that isn't hard. But this—' He sighed. 'I don't know.'

'How did you ever get in this state? Why don't you know him better?'

'You don't have to tell me that I'm to blame—'

'I'm not trying to apportion blame,' she insisted. 'I just want to help Joey. He seems to think I have the answers, but I don't really.'

'We were so proud of him when he was born,' Carson recalled. 'It was a few years before he began to lose some of his hearing.'

'He did have some hearing, then?'

'Yes. The doctor gave him a hearing aid, and we hoped that might do the trick. I thought Brenda was a good mother until things went wrong. Her career was taking off, and she didn't spend a lot of time with Joey, but she seemed to dote on him when she was here, and we had an excellent nanny.'

'How much time did you spend with him?' Gina asked gently.

'I was away a lot, building up the business. But when I came back—he grew so fast—if you could have seen him then—such a strong, clever child. Everybody envied us—'

He closed his eyes suddenly. Gina held her breath and didn't speak. She could tell that he'd gone away from her, back to the time when the world had been bright with hope, before calamity had fallen on him.

'I used to think about him as I was driving home,' he went on, still with his eyes closed. 'My little boy—my son—but better and stronger than me. He'd smile when he saw me, and I felt there was a secret understanding between us—a kind of promise for the future.'

He opened his eyes and saw her looking at him in consternation. 'I'm saying the wrong thing, aren't I? But I don't know why.'

She shook her head. It would take too long to tell him. Besides, didn't all new fathers see their sons as extensions of themselves? Valuing them as individuals came later. But in this case a tragedy had got in the way.

'What happened then?'

Carson threw himself back against the leather of the sofa and stared up at the ceiling.

'For a while he seemed to be doing well. He started to make sounds. Some of them even began to sound like words. He was fighting it. But he was losing. When we took him back to be assessed again we found his hearing had worsened. The answer was another hearing aid, stronger. But it happened again, and again. Always the power being turned up as his hearing slipped away, until, about a year ago, he became profoundly deaf. Now he hears nothing, and he's lost all the progress he seemed to have made.'

'So you stopped seeing him as a promise for the future,' she couldn't resist saying. 'And became ashamed of him.'

He sat up. 'Damn you, no! I was never ashamed of him.'

'Are you proud of him?' Gina asked remorselessly.

'How can I be—? I'm sorry for him.'

'Then don't be. Why should you pity him? He's got a really good brain. When he does finger-spelling, he never makes a mistake. Every word is spelled perfectly, even the difficult ones. How old is he, eight?'

'Nearly. In a few weeks.'

'Not even eight, and he has a reading age of at least twelve.'

'Yes, his teachers say the same. They all tell me how bright he is in a patronising way, as though that makes it all right. Can't any of you see that it makes it worse? It's a hard world out there. I've discovered that for myself. And he's going to have to survive in it. God knows how!'

She sighed, understanding his confusion. This was a man who'd fought to impose his will on the world, and largely succeeded. But only in business. Fate had given him a son who was poorly equipped for life's battles, and he didn't cope with that fact very well.

'Perhaps you'd better tell me a little about his school,' she suggested.

'He goes to a special place, near here, for children with disabilities. They've taught him signing and lip-reading, and they're supposed to teach him to talk as well, but he's not making much progress.'

She nodded thoughtfully. 'He talks almost like somebody who's never heard a human voice.'

'That's what baffles me. He must have heard something when he was young.'

'Yes, but he was too little to understand what he was hearing. When he was old enough to make the connection, the sounds had faded. I doubt if he remembers them now. So he never learned properly because children learn to talk by imitating what they hear.'

Privately she thought there might be another reason: that Joey, too old and wise for his years, had reacted to his mother's desertion and his father's incomprehension by abandoning the effort to talk and retreating into his own world—a world of water, sharks and shells, where he was king.

But she kept this to herself. It would be cruel to throw it at Carson when he was struggling to do better. And she already knew that Joey could be tempted out by someone he saw as a friend.

'It'll take time, and encouragement,' she said carefully. 'If he knows that you don't like the way he talks, he's got no incentive to try.'

'How can he possibly know?'

'Do you really think he hasn't sensed it? He knows a

lot more about you than you do about him. What a pity you haven't taken more interest in him.'

'How dare you say I take no interest in him? He's had the very best of everything—'

Gina lost patience. 'I'm sure he's had the best that money could buy,' she said sharply. 'It's a pity you can't buy parents, so that he could have had the best of them, too.'

As soon as the words were out she was shocked at herself for losing control of her tongue. And bewildered. It wasn't like her to fly off the handle so easily, but when she was defending Joey her anger flared up quickly.

Carson was looking at her, not angrily, but with a wry expression.

'I'm sorry,' she told him. 'I shouldn't have said that.'

'No, don't spoil it. I appreciate plain speaking, and I guess that hair of yours comes at a price.'

'Nonsense!' she said, colouring. 'It's just hair. It doesn't mean anything.'

'Well, I never met any blondes or brunettes who put me in my place like you do. And it's not "just hair". It's a glowing beacon, and it's beautiful. As I say, there's a price, but I don't mind paying it.'

'Can we drop this subject?' she asked frostily.

'If it bothers you to be told that you're beautiful.'

'This isn't about me.'

'What about your boyfriend with the spark plugs? Does he tell you that you're beautiful?'

'No, he says—' She checked, wondering at herself. It was fatal to answer him.

'Says what?' Carson persisted.

'That I'm reliable,' she admitted unwillingly.

'Oh, boy! He's really sweeping you off your feet, isn't he?'

Her lips twitched. 'I *am* reliable.'

'I'm sure you are, but as a loverlike tribute it lacks something, don't you agree?'

'Well, Dan is very much taken up with his business. In fact, he's rather like you.'

'He's not at all like me,' Carson muttered. 'Are you in love with him?'

'I—I'm not sure. I've known Dan for years. His mother taught me signing when I was a little girl. He was in and out of the house, and we became friends. He didn't mind my being deaf. He was used to people like that.'

'But what about now?'

'How do you mean?'

'You make him sound as though he was just a habit.'

'Well, some habits can be very nice,' she said defensively.

'Sure they can. But don't you want more?'

More, she thought. More than dear, dull, kindly, blinkered Dan?

She saw Carson watching her, and suddenly she felt self-conscious. There was something in his eyes that hadn't been there before, something dark and uncontrollable. It ignored the restraints she'd built so carefully into her life. It was reckless and magical. It made her blood sing and her heart beat powerfully.

More.

'I've never asked too much out of life,' she said after a while. 'Then you're not disappointed.'

'To hell with that! It's a philosophy for cowards. Take risks. Be disappointed. Then pick yourself up and go on to the next thing.'

'That's your philosophy. But not everyone can live like you.'

'Of course they can. There are no restraints except those you put on yourself.' He checked himself suddenly. 'Hell! I'm talking ignorant nonsense, aren't I?'

'A bit,' Gina said, smiling.

'For Joey, there are restraints he didn't put there himself. And for you. Why do you let me go on spouting rubbish?'

'Could I stop you?' she asked lightly.

He gave a rueful grin. 'Probably not. Let's call it a day before I say anything worse.'

CHAPTER FIVE

IT DIDN'T take Gina long to find that nature had intended Joey to be a little devil. If his deafness hadn't damaged his confidence he would have been a real handful. He was still sometimes possessed by an imp of mischief, but had enough charm to win forgiveness.

He reacted to the news that they were going to visit Mrs Saunders by sticking his lower lip out and sitting down, giving Gina a defiant look.

'We're going to the hospital,' she said firmly. 'Now!'

He eyed her, sizing up the strength of the opposition.

'Why don't you like her?' Gina asked.

Because she doesn't like me.

Gina knew better than to say, Nonsense, I'm sure she does. Instead, she put a friendly hand on his shoulder. 'Come on. Let's do our duty and get it over with.'

He made a face. Gina immediately made the same face back, and they laughed together.

They found Mrs Saunders sitting up in a chair. She was middle-aged and looked bruised and belligerent. She eyed Joey with wary hostility. He eyed her back in the same spirit.

'I don't want any of his tantrums in here,' were her first words.

'He doesn't have tantrums—' Gina began.

'That's what you think. Screaming and yelling—'

'Only because he can't make himself understood. It gets too much for him. When you come back—'

67

'I'm not coming back. I've got a new job waiting for me when I come out of here.'

'What?'

'I took the day off last week to go to an interview. The next day they called and asked me back for another interview. I was coming home from that when I had the accident.'

'So that's why you went out and left him alone,' Gina said angrily.

'Well, I could hardly take him with me, could I? Anyway, I've got another job and that's that.' She set her chin.

There was nothing to do but leave. From Joey's cheerful expression, Gina guessed he'd picked up the gist of the conversation.

For the rest of the day Gina was thoughtful. A plan was taking shape in her mind. At last she nodded to herself, confident that she had a way to make this work. When Carson called to say he would be late that evening she told him not to worry. She had everything in hand. He hung up with an easy mind.

So his shock was all the greater when he arrived home at ten o'clock that evening and found Gina's bags packed and standing in the living room.

'I was just going to take them out to my peanut,' she explained.

'You're not leaving?' he asked in alarm.

'Right now.'

'You can't do that.'

'I can. I don't care what arrangement you've made with my employers. If they fire me, they fire me. I've made up my mind.'

'Gina, just until Mrs Saunders comes back—'

'She isn't coming back. She's got another job—'

Carson swore under his breath. 'All right. I'll find someone else. But until then—'

'Joey doesn't need someone else. He needs his father. You're his father. Not me. Not Mrs Saunders. Not someone you hire from an agency, but you.'

'I've got a business to run—'

'The business is just an excuse because you can't face being alone with him.'

'Only because I know I'm no use to him.'

'Well, that can change, can't it? You can work on yourself until you are of use to him.'

'How?'

'You could learn sign language, for a start, so that you two can communicate. You should have done it long ago.'

'What time do you think I have—?'

'I'm disappointed in you, Carson. I thought you were an honest man, honest with yourself as well as everyone else.'

'Are you saying I'm not?'

'Why don't you admit the real reason you haven't learned sign language?'

'You're sure you know the real reason, are you?'

'You're asking me that, with my background?'

'All right. Tell me.'

'Because you can't face the truth. Learning to sign would have been an admission that your son is deaf. You probably decided not to admit it long ago. Shut your mind and it isn't true. That's it, isn't it?'

'Maybe,' he admitted, tight-lipped.

'But Joey can't put it aside like that. For him it *is* true, every moment of every day and night. There's no escape. He's trapped in a cage and all your money and success can't break down the door and pull him out of it. You can only get in there with him, and maybe lead him part of the way out. If you won't do that, I'm out of here.'

They faced each other. 'This is blackmail,' he said at last.

'Yes, it is.'

'Just give me a little time—'

'The time is *now*. My terms are simple. I want your promise about several things. Joey has six weeks of the summer holiday ahead of him. You've got to make use of that time. You learn sign language, and talk to him. And listen to him. He's very interesting.

'Plus you leave work early—no more getting home at ten. If meetings overrun, you cut them short. You take at least a week off to give him a holiday somewhere. I want your solemn word. If I don't get it, I leave this minute. And when Joey wakes up tomorrow you can explain my absence in any way you can.'

'And what would that do to him? I thought you wanted to help him.'

'I'm helping him the best way I know. Do I have your word, or shall I get my coat?'

Silence.

'You warned me you were tough,' he said.

'I had to be. You'll discover that Joey's tough too, for the same reason.'

'No prizes for guessing whose side you're on.'

'Carson, I see that little boy facing crippling problems with humour and courage. And I see his father, ducking out. Whose side do you expect me to take?'

'If I give you those promises, I want one in return.'

'What?'

'That you'll stay with us the whole six weeks. I can do it, Gina, but not without you.'

'If my employers say yes.'

'They will.'

She smiled. She knew she'd won. 'Yes, I'm sure they will, if you say so. All right. I promise if you do.'

He held out his hand. 'Shake.'

'Shake.'

He gripped her in an echo of their first handclasp. It had been only a few days ago, but they both felt as though they'd travelled a million miles.

'I've got a meal for you,' she said prosaically.

Over supper her mood was euphoric. She poured his wine and raised her own in salute. It was the salute of a victor.

'I'd hate to face you in the boardroom,' he grumbled. 'You'd bankrupt me in a week.'

'We ought to establish some ground rules.'

'Not bankruptcy. Take-over.'

'Who cleans this house?'

'Mrs Saunders used to do it, but I'm not asking you.'

'Good. My time belongs to Joey. I'll contact an agency and get someone to come in.'

'Anything you say.'

Over the second glass of wine, he said, 'You'd better tell me about sign language.'

'There's two kinds. Finger-spelling, which has a different sign for every letter. But it would take too long to spell every word out, so some words have signs of their own. Like this.'

She flattened her hand, fingers together and thumb apart, and laid it on her breast. Then she swept it down and up in a circle until it lay on her breast again.

'That's the sign for "please". Try it.'

He did so, awkwardly.

'No, keep your thumb separate,' she advised.

This time he got it right.

'Your first word,' she said proudly. 'If you spelled it out with your fingers it would look like this.'

She showed him, making each letter separately. 'There are signs for most words, so that you talk fast.'

'That sounds like an awful lot of signs to learn.'

'Don't tell me the man who built up Page Engineering doubts his own ability to learn something his little son can do?'

'Very clever! Do you take this approach with Joey?'

'I don't have this much trouble with Joey. He's bright as a button, and he never doubts that he can do things. That's half the battle.'

He grinned, and she felt an obscure disturbance within her. 'All right, teacher. On with the lesson.'

She laughed at him. She was still high from her victory.

'It'll come easier than you think,' she said. 'And you'll have Joey to help you.'

'If you imagine I'm going to let him see me fumbling—'

'Give me patience! Carson, Joey will be thrilled that you're doing this for him, and if you let him teach you it'll make him happier than anything.'

'Hmm!'

She could tell that the thought of being seen at a disadvantage was still hard for him to cope with, so she wisely didn't press the matter.

'Anyway, you'll master the signs, but you need the alphabet as well, because some words are too complicated for just one sign.'

'Then it's about time I started learning my alphabet.'

She held up her hand. 'A-B-C—'

He followed her carefully, until he could get as far as

M, without prompting. To his chagrin, that was as much as he could master in one evening, but Gina seemed pleased.

'What would you do if I went halfway and then broke my word?' he said. 'About the holiday, for instance?'

She gave him a curious smile. 'Funnily enough, it never once occurred to me that you'd go back on your word. Was I wrong?'

'No, you weren't wrong. It's rather alarming that you understand me so well.' He thought for a moment. 'I've got a friend who owns a travel agency. It's late to be booking Disneyland but he'll be able—no?' For Gina was shaking her head. 'Not Disneyland?'

'Not Disneyland. Kenningham.'

'Kenningham? That little seaside resort on the west coast? It's a dump.'

'It's got the best aquarium in the country. We could spend two days there, then go on to the second best aquarium. You know what Joey's interests are. Or I should say "interest", singular, because it's all he cares about. I shouldn't be surprised if one day he makes a real contribution to marine science.'

'Right,' he said, with the barest touch of scepticism in his voice.

'Carson, I'm serious. Joey is deaf, not stupid. His problem is that when he tries to talk he *sounds* stupid, but you've got to get beyond that. He has a first-class brain.' She tried a lighter note. 'Could Carson Page's son have anything else?'

He looked at her curiously. 'You're not just telling me this because you think he has to be bright before I can love him?'

'Have I said that?'

'You think it.'

'Is it true?'

'No, it isn't,' he said shortly. 'You may not think so but I love my son very much. Give me your glass. I'll refill it.'

This was so clearly a way of changing the subject that she didn't pursue it. Carson loved his son, but woe betide anyone who tried to talk about it. She was more convinced than if he'd made a long speech.

She sipped her wine before saying thoughtfully, 'Tell me, what do you know about wrasse?'

'Nothing. What is it?'

'Joey knows all about wrasse. He can talk about them for hours.'

'Them? Not it?'

'Right.'

'I feel as if I've walked into a madhouse.'

'The point is, wrasse is something you ought to know about.'

'Something to do with marine life?' he hazarded, clutching at straws.

'That's right.'

'I'll find out—'

'No, don't. Joey's an expert. Let him tell you.'

'Will that—make him happy?'

He was studying her face carefully, as a man might watch an unpredictable creature that could spring either way. Somewhere there was a key to this conversation, but only she had it.

'Very happy,' she told him.

'Then I'll do it.'

'But no looking it up. That's cheating. Let him tell you.'

'Whatever you say.'

He watched her for a moment as she leaned forward

to put down her wineglass. Her hair swung free, and after a moment he reached out to gently ease it back, revealing a tiny device behind her ear.

'Is that the implant you told me about?' he asked.

'That's right. There's a bit more actually inside my ear. It needs an operation to put it there.'

'And it cures your deafness?'

'No, I'm still deaf. If this is switched off I can't hear any more than Joey. But if it's on I can discern noises and understand them. Not exactly as you do, but enough for a normal life.'

'I don't understand. How can you hear and still be deaf?'

'In hearing people, the sound comes into the outer ear, crosses the inner ear and makes contact with the auditory nerve. But if the hairs of the inner ear aren't working, then they can't pick up the sound and transmit it to the nerve. A cochlear implant stimulates the hairs electrically instead of accoustically, and the sound gets passed on that way. I'm surprised Joey's specialist didn't mention implants to you a year ago.'

Carson grimaced. 'He kind of did, when we realised that Joey was finally deaf. I don't think I took much in. I was so shattered, I was blocking out a good deal. Besides, it seemed such a terrifying operation, drilling through his skull.

'We put it on hold—just for a while, we thought. But then Joey caught pneumonia. He's always been liable to chest infections. And after that he got every bug going— colds, flu, bronchitis. For months it was as if he finished one thing and started another. The doctor said he couldn't think of operating until Joey had put all that behind him.'

'And now?'

'Now he's well and strong again, so perhaps—do you really think—?' His face was suddenly as full of eagerness as his son's when something pleased the child. The likeness made Gina smile.

'Maybe,' she said. 'It might be time to take him back to the specialist and have him assessed for one of these. But, Carson, please don't pin your hopes on this. Not everyone is suitable. But it's worth finding out. If it's going to happen, I'd like it to be while I'm around.'

'He might be able to hear,' Carson said slowly, 'and talk—'

'Eventually. He'd have to learn to talk from scratch, like a baby does, only he'll find it hard because he's older.

'I was lucky because I learned to talk before I went deaf and that helps a lot. When I started hearing sounds again I could remember what they meant. But Joey hardly had any chance to hear sounds, so he'll need to learn them all from the beginning before he can start to speak. Joey will need speech therapy and it'll take time—at least a year, maybe longer.' She gave him a mischievous look. 'So you'll still need to learn that signing, to communicate with him in the meantime.'

'You're the boss!'

'Give me the details of his specialist and I'll fix a meeting.'

'All right. I'm in your hands.' After a moment he added, 'Perhaps that's the best place to be.'

He saw her upstairs and together they looked in on Joey, who was sleeping deeply. When Carson had bid her goodnight he went to his own room, thoughtful.

His head was full of Gina, but he couldn't make out which one. There seemed to be so many of her.

He'd met her first as the sweet, funny, slightly crazy

girl who'd dented his car. She'd charmed him, but it had been an hour's fleeting delight.

When they'd seen each other again, everything had been different. She'd met Joey in circumstances that had made her condemn Joey's father, and before Carson's eyes she'd changed into an avenging fury. The sun she'd briefly shone on him had vanished, replaced by thunder and lightning.

Now there was another Gina, practically a school-marm, telling him that he would do this and that—or else! He grinned slightly at the memory.

It amazed him that she saw herself as a little brown mouse. Because, of course, she wasn't a mouse at all. For Joey's sake she would take on the whole world. She'd taken on Carson Page without trouble, he reflected wryly. He didn't know how all this was going to end, but deep instinct told him it could end well—although whether only for Joey, or for himself as well, he still wasn't sure.

Being Carson Page, he arrived home next day with printed sheets showing signs and finger-spelling.

'I tried to make a start,' he told Gina. 'I even practised a couple of letters in my office but my secretary came in and saw me doing it. She gave me the oddest look.'

'Won't she just assume you're doing it for your deaf son?'

'She doesn't know. Nobody does.' She was silent and he challenged her angrily, 'Say it!'

'Nobody must know that Carson Page did something less than perfectly,' she said, angry in her turn.

His temper flared. He was doing his best, dammit, but she wouldn't give him any credit. 'By God, you're a hard, judgemental woman!'

He stormed out, not looking where he went, and collided with Joey in the doorway, so hard that the child fell and Carson nearly lost his balance.

Joey got up quickly and made a sign, folding his hand with the thumb protruding at the top. He touched his chest, circled away and back to his chest.

'What's he saying?' Carson asked tensely.

'That sign means "sorry",' Gina told him.

'But it was my fault.'

'Then tell him that you're sorry. It's not a difficult sign.'

Joey began to apologise again, but Carson seized his hand and stopped him. Slowly he folded his own fingers over, thumb protruding, laid his hand on his chest, made the circular movement. Into Joey's eyes came a look of total mystification. It hurt Carson to see it. He repeated the sign. *Sorry.*

Joey frowned, turning his head slightly on one side. An apology from his father was something he simply didn't understand.

'Have you never apologised to him before?' Gina asked.

Carson could hardly speak. 'I don't think—I ever have.' He was finding Joey's 'silence' agonising.

At last the silence was broken. A happy smile broke over the child's face. He touched his father's hand, stilling it as Carson had stilled his. *It's all right.*

Carson drew a long breath. Something had just happened that had shaken him. If you blinked you might have missed it, but it was like a volcano inside. For a moment the roles had been reversed, and the little boy had been the adult, reassuring him that they would manage somehow.

But then, before his eyes, his son withdrew from him.

The unfamiliar intimacy had embarrassed him, and he became an ordinary little boy.

'Let's have supper,' Gina said, reading the situation without trouble.

Joey's attention had been caught by the papers with the finger alphabet. He looked at them, then at his father, his eyebrows slightly raised in a query.

'Why don't you tell him that you're learning?' Gina asked.

'I don't know the signs for that yet.'

'Try saying it. He's good at lip-reading. Put yourself where he can see your mouth, and speak clearly.'

Carson positioned himself, his face on a level with Joey's. 'I'm learning signs, so that we can talk.'

Joey frowned. He hadn't quite caught it.

'Slower,' Gina advised.

This time they did better. Joey opened his hand, fingers together, thumb apart, and touched his chin once.

'That means "good",' Gina said. 'You do it. It's quite easy.'

'Thanks for the vote of confidence,' he said with a faint grin. He signed, *Good.*

'Haven't you spoken to him in the past?' she asked as they laid the table.

'I've tried, but he never seemed to understand me.'

'Maybe you weren't trying hard enough.'

'You sound like a schoolmistress,' he grumbled. 'Yes, miss. Will try harder.'

'See that you do,' she told him with mock severity.

'And when he did follow what I was saying he tried to answer and—I don't know.'

'He made those sounds that you can't bear to hear,' she finished remorselessly.

He took a deep breath. 'You really sock it to a man right between the eyes, don't you?'

'No point in any other way. Are you going to give up?'

'I didn't get where I am today by giving up.'

'And where are you today, Carson?' she asked coolly.

He was about to lecture her about Page Engineering and its place in the commercial world, but stopped himself in time. Of course, she wasn't talking about that.

Nothing that he'd done impressed her, he realised. His glittering achievements were as nothing beside his failure with his son.

Joey's pleasure in his father's efforts led to him being a little carried away. Over the meal he tried to talk to him, spelling, making signs, and going too fast for Carson to follow.

'Slow down,' Carson begged at last. 'I'm only a beginner.'

Joey nodded and repeated the sign he was demonstrating. It was complex, and Carson got it wrong. Frowning, he tried again, making a sound of impatience when it eluded him. He wasn't used to not being able to do things well. Then Joey laid a hand over his father's and gently moved the fingers into the right position.

'Thank you,' Carson said, in words. Joey frowned, watching his mouth. 'Thank you,' Carson repeated.

Understanding dawned. Joey flattened his hand, touched his chin with it, moved it away. He was watching Carson closely to see if he followed this. Carson looked at Gina, but she wouldn't help him.

'Does that mean—"thank you"?' he asked uncertainly. She nodded, pleased.

She was glad to slip into the background while father and son made the first tentative steps to knowing each other better. It went well, and by the time they both put him to bed she knew that Carson was feeling happier.

Later that night, as they parted outside her door, Carson said, 'What was that sign Joey made you the first night—when he said he liked you?'

Gina formed her hand into the Y shape.

'This means "like". You do the rest by pointing at yourself and the other person.'

He tried it, and managed the shape.

'That's it,' she encouraged.

He pointed at himself, formed the Y, then pointed at her.

'You've got it.' Gina made the gesture back. 'I—like—you.'

He did it again, saying, 'I—like—you.'

Then something seemed to strike him, making him uneasy. He said, 'Goodnight,' hurriedly, and walked off.

CHAPTER SIX

GINA prepared the ground carefully for everything she had to say to Joey, waiting for exactly the right moment to present itself. In the end Joey made the moment happen with a practical joke.

Walking through the door of his room, one evening, she was pulled up short by a stream of cold water over her. He'd put a vase on top of the door.

'Joey!' That was Carson, just behind her, outraged on her behalf.

Gina silenced him with a swift gesture. The little boy was doubled up with laughter at the success of his antics, and she joined him, seizing him up in a ruthless embrace and swinging him around.

'Wretch!' she said. 'Horrible little wretch!'

Rightly understanding this as a term of affection, Joey laughed harder than ever.

'It's a bit unkind, after all you've done for him,' Carson grumbled, picking up the vase.

'It's a joke,' Gina protested. 'He's a little boy. Little boys make jokes. But look, darling—'

Carson's spine prickled, then he realised that 'darling' had been addressed to Joey.

'Look, darling, next time—'

'Next time?' Carson demanded.

'Hush! Next time, don't use water. Look.' She showed him the speech processor that was attached to her implant. 'That's what I use so that I can hear. It mustn't get wet or it won't work any more.'

It was amazing how quickly Joey was transformed from a little boy to a serious person dealing with something he understood.

Hearing aid, he signed.

'No, it's much more than that. A hearing aid is for people who can hear a little, and it makes it louder. This is for people who are completely deaf—like us.'

At the word 'us', Joey raised his head and stared at her. At the start, Gina had told him she was deaf, but she could so obviously hear that he'd vaguely assumed she was talking about the past. His father watched him with bated breath.

But you're not deaf any more?

'Yes, I am. I'm as deaf as you. But with this—' she touched it '—I can hear.'

He grew agitated. *Did I damage it?*

'No, I was lucky. The water didn't touch it. And if it was wet I could always get another. But no more vases of water.'

He shook his head vigorously. *Promise.*

Then he frowned again and looked wistfully at the device. *Can I have one?*

'We could find out.'

Yes, please. Joey's eyes were shining. To him this was a dream come true. How well she knew that feeling! She held him tightly, praying that his dreams really would come true.

'Have you contacted the specialist yet?' Carson asked.

'I wrote to him today.'

'Wouldn't a phone call be quicker?'

'I don't always find telephones easy. Sometimes it's unavoidable and it's not too bad with someone whose voice I've heard before. But with strangers it's often easier to write. When I'm in the office Dulcie helps me out.'

'How did you manage that time with Brenda?'

'Funnily enough, I had no problems with her. Some voices are like that.'

She received the answer the next day. Setting up the appointment was the easy part. The hard part was explaining to Joey the number of people who must assess him before he was declared suitable. She told him that it would take several days of hard work, that he might find tiring. He nodded and shrugged to show that he regarded this as no big deal. He was like a small determined scientist, intent on getting an experiment right.

Carson came with them to the hospital. It was obvious to Gina that he was far more nervous than his son. Joey was excited but happy. He seemed to have no doubts about the outcome of his assessment, and he was proved right. The operation was set for two days ahead.

On the morning he was due to go into the hospital Joey was in high spirits, demanding that Gina should tell him her own story.

'But I've told you a dozen times,' she protested.

Again, please. He had a way of signing 'please' with great vigour, which exactly captured the quality of a child's imploring voice. She smiled and began a story that seemed to delight him more every time he heard it.

'I could hear until I was about your age. Then I had a very bad fever and, when I recovered, I was completely deaf. They didn't have cochlear implants in those days, so I stayed as I was for ten years.

'During that time they were developed, and at last it happened. I had the operation that you'll have tomorrow, and then I had to wait four weeks for it to heal before they could attach the speech processor to the outside.'

Four whole weeks!

She smiled tenderly. 'It'll pass, darling.'

She went into the hospital with him that evening, staying in a connected room. Carson came later on that evening and found them watching television, reading the subtitles and giggling at a comedian. Joey was eating a hearty supper which seemed to consist mainly of ice cream.

'He can't have anything after midnight tonight,' Gina explained. 'So he's making the most of it.'

She slipped away to let them be alone together. Carson's signing had greatly improved, and he could cope with a basic conversation now, if only he could think of what to say to his son.

He emerged in half an hour. 'The nurse told him it was time for bed. He says he can't sleep until you're there.'

'I'll go right along. There's plenty for you to eat at home—'

'No need; I'm going back to work. I'll get a snack. Call me tomorrow when he's out of surgery.'

'But—'

'You'd better go to Joey. He's getting impatient.'

He strode off down the corridor and pushed through the swing doors without looking back. Gina was left with a little desolate ache in her heart. It was plain that Carson wanted to get out of there as soon as possible. His whole air since he'd arrived had been tense and unhappy.

Of course, some men just disliked hospitals. But that was no use to Joey, she thought, hardening her heart. Why did Carson have to disappoint her just now, when she'd begun to think—that was, to hope—?

She pulled herself together and returned to Joey's room.

Next morning found him calm and happy. He smiled as he was given his premedication, and gave her a drowsy wave as he was wheeled away.

There was nothing she could do but wait, and the hours that stretched ahead seemed endless. She thought of Carson attending meetings, giving orders, increasing his profits, imagining that he'd done all that was needed because he'd bought his son the best treatment in the best hospital. She almost hated him.

'Gina,' said a quiet voice.

Carson was standing in the door of her room. His face was very pale and there were shadows under his eyes.

'Can I come in here?' he asked tentatively. 'Is it all right?'

'Yes, of course.'

'Is there any news?'

'No, he's still in surgery. You don't look very well yourself.'

He sat heavily beside her on the sofa. 'I've felt better. I had to leave work; I was useless. I couldn't concentrate. Simmons, my deputy, kept droning on about something or other and asking how I intended to resolve the problem. I couldn't even remember what the problem was.'

'Couldn't you?' she asked tenderly. Inside her a well spring of happiness had shot up.

'It seemed so unimportant. Why were they going on about nothing, while my son…?'

His hands were shaking. Gina enclosed them in both of hers and he held onto her so tightly that it was painful.

'In the end I told Simmons to do whatever he damned well pleased, because I was leaving. They all looked at me as though I was crazy.'

'Good for you!' she said softly.

He gave a shaky laugh. 'I think that must be the first word of approval you've ever given me.'

'Well, you deserved it.'

'I couldn't bear being in this place yesterday evening. It all matters so much—it's his one big chance—his whole life—everything. I want to give him the world but—the one thing that counts—just you— I'm talking gibberish, aren't I?'

'It doesn't matter. I'm good at filling in the gaps.'

'Yes, of course. Thank God for you! I couldn't sleep last night. I kept thinking about you—and him—seeing the night out in this place, and being so brave. And all I did was run. I told myself that you were both better off without me, and it's true—'

'No, it isn't,' she said softly. 'Joey clings to me a little more because I've been through this, but you're his father. I'm glad you're here.'

'Are you? Honestly?'

'Honestly.' She winced.

'What's the matter?'

'My hands. You're crushing them.'

'I'm sorry.' He began to rub her hands between his own. 'Is that better?'

'A bit. Give them a little more.' It felt good to have her slight hands enveloped in his large ones. They were powerful hands, almost predatory, and in business she supposed he was a predator. But now he was merely a vulnerable father, seeking comfort and also giving it.

He stopped rubbing and his shoulders sagged suddenly. 'Will it be long?' he asked in agony.

'I'm afraid so. It's a very delicate operation, just behind his ear.'

'Dear God!' He dropped his head into his hands. 'What can I do for him?'

'You've done it by coming here. Just wait, and be there for him when he awakes.'

'Just wait? I don't know how. The fact is that if I can't give orders or write letters I'm pretty useless.' He gave a short laugh full of derision against himself. 'You've always thought I was useless, haven't you?'

'For a little while I saw you through a distorting glass—'

'No, you didn't. You saw me as I am,' he said bitterly.

'Carson, don't beat yourself up like this. It won't help Joey if you fret yourself into a breakdown.'

'Me? I won't have a breakdown. I've always been strong. I'm famous for it. The powerful Carson Page who could flatten his enemies with a stroke. And all the time the really strong one was my little boy, fighting his battles without any help from me. I can't even tell him that I love him. He doesn't care whether I do or not—'

'That's not true.'

'Isn't it? You saw how he drew back from me, that time I tried to say sorry.'

'He's in new territory, just as you are. You two still need to get to know each other. Don't hurry it. Take it at his pace.'

'You must be the wisest woman on earth. How did I manage before you came into my life? Well, I didn't manage, did I?'

'You managed to build up a commercial empire.'

'As though that mattered twopence! *Oh, dear God!*'

Suddenly he dropped his head into his hands again. Gina slipped her arms around him and rested her head against him.

'I'm here,' she said softly.

She felt his hand seek hers, and they sat without moving. Gina was twisted into a slightly uncomfortable position, but she wouldn't shift in case Carson released her and moved away. She didn't want that. She wanted to go on sitting here, feeling his warmth and heaviness against her, knowing that she was necessary to him, and enjoying that knowledge so much that it scared her.

After a while his breathing changed and she realised that he had drifted into a doze. She wondered about the night he'd passed in that empty house with only his fear and sorrow for company. She'd had to stay with Joey, of course, but the child wasn't the only one who needed her. And Carson's agonies had been plainly written on his face when he'd come in. Now he was simply worn out by dread and sleeplessness.

She must have dozed off herself because she was startled by the sound of the door to Joey's room being opened and pulled wide to let the hospital bed be wheeled through. She gave Carson a gentle shake.

'They're coming back,' she said. 'It's over.'

They stood together in the door of her room while the nurses got to work settling Joey. Through the bustle they could get only a slight glimpse of the tiny figure on the bed, his head swathed in bandages. Carson tried to take a step forward but Gina restrained him.

'Let them do their job,' she said.

A young woman in a white coat approached them. 'I'm Dr Henderson,' she said. 'Everything went very well. He'll be coming round in an hour.'

Carson closed his eyes. 'Thank God!'

At last everyone left except for one nurse, who stood back to let them approach the bed, one on each side. Joey lay very still, breathing evenly. He looked small and frail, but Gina noticed that his colour was good. She kissed him briefly, then moved away, leaving Carson alone with his son.

He leaned down towards the child and stroked his face. She saw his lips move, and turned away, aching for him, for she thought she knew what he had said.

In three days Joey was home, trying to be patient for the weeks that must pass before he could hope to hear his first sounds. The bandages were off, leaving his head looking the same except for a shaved patch beneath his left ear, and a dressing.

On the surface life went on as before. After the intimacy they'd shared in the hospital it seemed to Gina that something must have changed between herself and Carson. But, having briefly emerged from his shell, he'd retreated back into it. Perhaps he felt he'd given away too much of his inner self, and now wanted to turn away from her, and deny it. Whatever the reason, it made her sad. But there was nothing she could do.

She saw little of him, given that they were sharing a house. He came home early, and the three of them ate together, before she put Joey to bed. He would look in to say goodnight to his son, and it delighted her to see that they were more relaxed with her now.

After that Carson worked in his study, spending hours on the telephone to countries in different time zones. He was often still working when she went to bed.

But one night she stayed up late to watch a long movie, and as it came to an end he joined her with brandy and two glasses. He poured one and set it down beside her before sprawling on the big leather sofa and letting out a long breath.

'I've just spent an hour on the phone to the stupidest man in creation,' he said with his eyes closed. 'You think you've cleared up one point, then he goes back to the beginning and starts again. After three times, you start losing the will to live.'

He drained his glass and poured more brandy. It was part of Carson's controlled nature that he never touched alcohol during the day, even at lunch. Especially at lunch. Let the others make mistakes because their wits were fuddled. Carson Page was always coldly alert to take advantage of them. But late at night, in his own home, he drank occasionally.

Gina sipped hers with pleasure. Normally she didn't care for alcohol, but this was a very fine vintage. 'One of those days?' she asked sympathetically.

'Don't get me started,' he groaned.

He gave her the grin of one comrade enjoying a grumble with another, and she was reminded of how he'd seemed to her on the first day, in the car park, exasperated but generous.

She couldn't help smiling at the picture he presented. Dealing with the stupidest man in creation had caused him to discard his tie, pull open his shirt and tear his hair until it was totally dishevelled.

He looked ten years younger at least, as far as Gina could see, for the only light came from one low reading lamp, and most of the room was in shadows.

'How was your day?' he asked, yawning. 'Joey seemed cheerful at supper.'

'Yes, we had a good time. We went to the park and took a boat on the lake. And we bumped into a teacher from his school. Alan Hanley. He seemed a nice man, and he filled in some gaps for me.'

'I've met him. How did Joey react?'

'Oddly, I thought. He was polite but they don't seem to get through to each other.'

'So what's your secret?'

'I beg your pardon?'

'Joey has learned from experts. Some of them are deaf, so they understand his problems too. But he's chosen you as the one person he can relate to. What do you have that the others don't?'

'I wish I knew,' she said. 'How can you explain empathy?'

'You can't, I guess. It's like love. It comes out of nowhere and it can't be explained.'

'And it seems to survive, no matter what people do to destroy it,' Gina mused.

'What does that mean?'

'Joey was talking about his mother today. Did you tell her about his operation, by the way?'

He shrugged. 'What would be the point?'

'I suppose you're right, but it's frightening how much he still loves her. I don't know what to say to him when he talks like that—whether to encourage him or discourage him.'

'She'll hurt him just as much either way,' Carson said. His head was thrown back against the side of the sofa, and he seemed to talk into the distance. Gina had noticed that he did this whenever the conversation veered towards the personal. It had the effect of a visor being pulled down to shield his eyes.

'Her great gift was always her charm,' he went on, looking up at the shadowed ceiling. 'Her beauty is almost secondary. She can charm the birds off the trees, and it works even when you know she can turn it on and off like a tap. You tell yourself that this time you'll be proof against it and then...' His voice trailed away into silence.

'Was it like that with you?' Gina ventured to ask.

He didn't reply at first, and she wondered if he was

offended. When he finally began to speak, it was as though he was talking to himself.

'At first, you think it's all for you, that you've been specially privileged with that enchanting look, the incredible smile, as though she's been waiting all her life to meet just you. After all, she's only nineteen, and how many wiles can she have learned at that age?

'You tell yourself all this because you're a young fool, madly in love, and you want to believe it. It's actually a kind of arrogance to think such a prize has fallen into your hands because you deserve it, but at that age you are arrogant. And you'll believe anything if she says it with that special smile. "Darling, I love you—only you—there'll never be anyone else—"'

'But she must have loved you, or why would she have married you?' Gina asked.

'She's a lady of large appetites, which I was able to satisfy,' Carson said bluntly. 'And when that kind of passion overwhelms you, and you're too callow and ignorant to know that passion isn't everything, you think it's enough. And when you discover it isn't—it's too late.'

He fell silent. Gina's heart was beating hard at this glimpse into Carson's secret pain, but she knew she was hearing things that weren't for her, things he would regret telling her later.

Soon she would yawn and say it was time for her to go to bed. This would cut off his confidences about the woman he'd once loved, and who still seemed to obsess him. And it was better for them both that it should be so.

The moments stretched on. She didn't move, and she knew she wasn't going to. She was doing this for Joey, she told herself. The more she knew about his background, the more she could help him.

But it wasn't for Joey's sake that she strained to catch every inflection of Carson's voice when he spoke of his ex-wife.

'I knew she wanted to be famous, when we married,' he went on, 'but I had no idea how her ambition possessed her. She seemed so happy as a wife and mother that I thought it would last. Later I realised that it was just a stage, something she wanted to try out, like a new role.'

He drained and refilled his glass again, as though it was only with the aid of alcohol that he could endure his memories.

'And when we discovered that Joey had problems she got tired of the role, and wanted something else. I tried to be understanding. We had a good nanny so that Brenda was free to spend time away from home. I didn't like her going, but I thought our marriage was strong enough to survive anything.' He gave a scornful laugh. 'I had some very naive notions in those days—true love conquers all—no mountain too high. All that stuff the songs tell you.'

'And you don't believe that now?' Gina asked, keeping her voice blank of expression.

'If ever a man and woman loved each other, we did. And it all fell apart like a shoddy toy. Infatuation is a bad basis for marriage. The best one is if people have something in common and are fond of each other—but, even then, not too fond.' He gave a grunt of bitter laughter. 'If I'd known that then, I'd never have married a woman I was crazy about and we'd have spared ourselves a lot of grief.

'She began spending longer and longer away. There

were film parts that took her abroad. The parts became better fairly quickly. She was sleeping her way to the top.

'At first she denied it. She can be so convincing. She can make you doubt what you know to be true. Then I caught her with someone—she begged me to forgive her—swore it would never happen again—'

'And you believed her?'

'It sounds crazy, doesn't it? But I needed to believe her for my own sanity. In the end she didn't bother to pretend any more, and I knew I had to cut her right out of my life, or go mad. So that's what I did.'

The last words had an air of finality, as though he'd drawn a line across a page. After that he said no more.

Gina sat, aghast at the demon that had been released. Beneath Carson's quiet words she sensed a wilderness of anguish and rage. He'd known a passion such as came to few people, and its destruction had left him a shell. He had 'cut her out'. And what was left behind was emptiness, because the only way to cut her out of his heart was to cut his heart out too.

A slight thud made her look up. His glass had slipped out of his hand and fallen to the carpet. He was asleep.

She bent to retrieve the glass, moving quietly so as not to awaken him. His head had fallen sideways and in the soft glow from the lamp Gina could see the relaxed lines of his face. With the trouble smoothed away by sleep he looked boyish, vulnerable.

She hadn't consciously noticed his mouth before, but now she saw how wide and firm it was, how sensual it must have been before cruel experience taught him to beware sensuality.

'She's a lady of large appetites, which I was able to

satisfy... When that kind of passion overwhelms you...you think it's enough.'

Bitter words from a bitter heart, about something he no longer believed in. Why should she care?

He presented a controlled face to the world because he dreaded to be overwhelmed again, but once he'd been happy to give himself up to his love. The thought was mysteriously painful.

As she knelt her face was so close to his that she could feel his breath brush her mouth softly. The effect on her was electric. He hadn't even touched her, and yet she felt the charge go through her body, melting it, making it weak with desire. She discovered that she was trembling.

She ought to go, but she stayed, thinking that somewhere in the world was a woman who'd had this man's passion and thrown it away. And wondering if that woman was mad.

If he had loved her she would never have left him—because it would have been like tearing out her own heart. His love would have been the pinnacle of her life, fulfilling every dream, satisfying every desire. Instinct too deep to be examined told her that.

She seemed to have been taken over by another will, one that held here there watching him yearningly, made her lean towards him when she knew she ought to leave. It kept her still, fighting the temptation to lay her lips gently against his, but not fighting it very hard. In another moment she would yield and kiss him. And never mind the consequences!

He stirred, muttered, reached out his hand blindly. It touched her face and she froze, terrified in case he awoke and found her there. It seemed like an age that she knelt motionless while his fingers lay against her lips and her heart thundered.

Gradually she took his hand between hers and moved it away from her face to lay it on the sofa. Then she rose to her feet and fled the room.

Carson opened his eyes with a start, wondering if he'd been sleeping or waking. In his twilight state he'd almost thought that...

But there was nobody there.

CHAPTER SEVEN

ALL this time Dan had been keeping in touch, regularly asking her for a date, but she'd put him off, using Joey as an excuse. But when the boy had been home for ten days Carson said, 'Dan called you again today. I shouldn't monopolise you the way I've been doing. Call him back and say you'll go out.'

'How will you manage alone with Joey?'

'Well enough. We can practise signs and he can have a good laugh at my expense. It's a pity you won't be here to see that.'

'Don't worry,' she said mischievously. 'He'll tell me all about it later.'

He grinned. 'I'll bet.'

His smile was cordial but it didn't invite her in. It never did, these days.

The morning after their talk he'd said casually, 'I had a drop too much last night. It always makes me come out with nonsense. That's why I don't do it often. Did I say much?'

'Hardly anything,' she'd assured him. 'You were half asleep.'

'Fine. Fine.' And the matter was closed.

Encouraged by the generous wage Carson was paying her, on top of her salary from Renshaw Baines, she splashed out on a new dress. She had her doubts as soon as she got it home. It was pale yellow chiffon, floaty and glamorous, and she couldn't imagine where Dan was likely to take her that would justify it.

It wasn't a Dan sort of dress at all, she realised as she paraded in front of the hall mirror, her own room being too small for parading. It was designed to bring out the depth of her eyes and the auburn glow of her hair, and he was too used to her to observe either. This was a dress for a man whose attention she wanted to claim so completely that he would forget all other women.

Joey sat on the stairs watching her. Laughing, she gave him a twirl and he made the sign for 'pretty'.

'Thank you, kind sir,' she said, curtseying before him.

'What did he say?' Carson was standing in the doorway, watching them. His eyes made her feel self-conscious. That happened often now, ever since the night he'd told her about Brenda, or before, when he'd turned to her in his anguish at the hospital. But then he'd turned away again.

'Oh—he likes it,' she said vaguely.

Joey signed the word again.

'Spell it for me,' Carson told him. Joey did so. 'Pretty? Right? Yes, Gina is very pretty.' Joey spelled vigorously. 'Very, very pretty,' Carson amended. 'Yes, she is. I think so too.'

He made a circular motion with his hand, and she twirled again. 'My son has good judgement,' he observed, his eyes on her. 'Very, very, *very* pretty.'

'Thank you,' she said, smiling and agitated together. Now she knew why she'd bought this flattering creation.

The truth was there as she regarded the vision in the mirror. And vision was the word. The elegant hair, the beautifully applied make-up. That had never been done for Dan and his spark plugs. In fact, Dan never noticed what she was wearing. But Carson noticed. She felt as though the breath had been knocked out of her.

The doorbell made her jump. Please don't let it be

Dan, she thought. She needed time to come to terms with her feelings.

But it was Dan. There was only a moment to pull herself together, but she did her best. Of course Carson had become important to her, she reasoned. She shared his roof, was involved with his life and his saddest secrets. A few hours in the fresh air of Dan's company would dispel the illusion that it was anything more.

Dan's eyes widened as he saw the lovely gown. And for once, she thought with relief, he'd noticed how she was dressed. He was even moved to comment.

'I say, you've glammed up a bit, haven't you? We're only going dog-racing, you know.'

'Dog-racing?' Carson enquired innocently.

'I thought we were having dinner,' Gina said in dismay.

'There's a restaurant overlooking the track where we can get a bite.'

'I'll go and change,' she said at once.

'No, don't do that. Time's running on and I don't want to miss the first race. You'll do as you are. Get your coat.'

As he closed the door behind them Carson looked at Joey. The boy might not be able to hear, but his father could tell that he'd picked up the atmosphere.

Their eyes met in a moment of pure masculine communication, for which no words or signs were needed.

What on earth does she see in *him*?

'You're doing a great job, I'll give you that,' Dan conceded generously. 'Have some more of this pie and peas. It's great.'

Gina adjusted a floaty end of chiffon so that it was out of danger. Pie and peas.

They'd found a place at the restaurant high over the track, with a window on one side, through which they could watch the races. Dan had bet on every race, won two, lost one, and was in good spirits.

'How do you know I'm doing a great job?' Gina asked. 'You barely saw Joey.'

'I meant with his father. Got him where you want him. He doubled his order with my firm today.'

'Did he, indeed?' she mused.

'Look, I know what you're thinking.'

'Bet you don't,' she said with an unconscious return to their childhood camaraderie.

'Bet I do. You're thinking he's only keeping me sweet to keep you doing his bidding.'

This was so exactly what she thought that she was reduced to silence. Dan was in a perceptive mood tonight. But then, Dan was always perceptive where spark plugs were concerned.

'They're good plugs, Gina. All I ask is the chance to prove it, and that's what you're giving me. I appreciate it. It can't be easy working as his unpaid nursemaid.'

'Not unpaid. He pays me on top of my salary from the firm. How do you think I could afford this dress?'

Down below, a race was about to start. Dan managed to tear his attention away long enough to study the beautiful garment.

'Hmm, yes. I can see it cost a packet. Pity to waste money, though. You could have—look, they're ready to start!'

'Dan—'

'Hang on, darling! I've got a bet on Silver Lad.'

For the next few minutes he was lost to her. And when Silver Lad had romped home it was hard to get him to talk about anything but his winnings. By the time she'd brought him back to the matter in hand the dogs were being led out for the next race.

'It's my lucky night. I've got a bet on Slyboots, the black dog on the far side. He's the favourite and the odds are only four to five, but never mind.'

'Yes, let's forget Slyboots. We have other things to think about. Dan, you're really extraordinary.'

'Am I, darling? That's very nice of you.'

'I mean, anyone else would kick up a fuss about my sharing a house with another man, but you don't turn a hair.'

'Well, there's nothing in it, is there?'

'No, there isn't,' she said with a little constraint. 'But why are you so sure?'

'Because I know you. You'd never even think of him in that way. You're doing this for us, and we make a fabulous team. They're dead pleased with me at work for landing such a big fish. I'm in line for a bonus, so maybe it's time we started planning the future.'

'The future?'

'Our future. Pipe and slippers, all that. Hey, they're off!'

She stared at him. 'Dan, is that a proposal?'

'What?'

She shouted to get his attention. *'Is that a proposal?'*

Above the din she had to lip-read his answer. 'If you like.'

I don't like, she thought crossly. I don't want to be proposed to over pie and peas, by a man who's giving half his attention to whether the favourite is going to come in at four to five.

But this was Dan, who hadn't changed since she'd known him. He was still the same well-meaning, emotionally dense dinosaur he'd always been. It was she who had changed. What had been enough once wasn't enough now.

He drove her home in a state of euphoria at having had four winners. He didn't seem to notice that she hadn't answered his proposal—such as it was. Perhaps he thought no answer was needed.

As they drew up outside the house Gina braced herself to say what she must. For this was where Dan would kiss her goodnight, and she knew that she couldn't let him do it. She didn't want Dan's lips on hers, or any man's, except—

'The lights are on. He's still up,' he said. 'Let's get in quickly, then you slip away and make us some coffee so that I get a real chance to talk to him.'

As she let them both into the house she could just see Carson through the open door of his office. The sound of the door made him look up, and he came out into the hall. Amid the conventional remarks about a pleasant evening, Gina noticed Joey peering through the banisters at her.

'That's the fifth time he's been down to see if you're back,' Carson said.

'Why don't you go and put him back to bed, darling?' Dan said promptly.

And give Dan his chance, she thought. But there was no resisting the delight in Joey's face, so she mounted the stairs, smiling, to receive his ecstatic, relieved welcome.

Left alone with a determined Dan, Carson bowed to the inevitable and shepherded him into the kitchen for coffee.

'So, you had a good evening?'

'Great time. Won a packet.'

'And Gina?'

'She had a couple of winners, too.'

'I meant, did she enjoy herself?'

'Oh, yes. That's the great thing about Gina. Easy to please. Never makes trouble.'

'Yes, that would be a great advantage in a woman,' Carson said, eyeing him oddly. He had no fear that Dan would notice the tension in his voice, and he was right.

'That's what I say. Gina and I make a good team. In fact, I said so to her tonight, and she agreed. Well, it's time we were settling things.'

Carson paused, his hand halfway to the coffee pot. 'You mean—?'

'Bound to get hitched, one day. Been on the cards for years. Never wanted anyone else. She's a dear little thing.'

'Yes,' Carson murmured.

He placed two cups on the table. It gave him something to do with his hands. Then the sugar, the milk. Pour the coffee. Do something. Keep busy. Anything to hide the fact that he'd just been badly shaken up.

'Thought I'd take her out to buy a ring. Not that I go much for that sort of fiddle-faddle, but girls seem to like it. Tomorrow evening is all right with you, is it?'

'Perfectly all right,' Carson said coolly.

When Gina came down she found the two men discussing business in the kitchen. Carson was at his most urbane, flattering Dan with attention.

'I'm grateful to you for being understanding about Gina's presence here. My son's needs are so great—'

'Poor little tyke,' Dan said with automatic sympathy. 'If he needs Gina, of course she must stay.'

'Exactly,' Carson agreed. 'She's trying to give Joey the kind of perfect care and understanding her own mother gave her.'

Dan gave a yelp of laughter. 'Perfect care and understanding? Whatever gave you that idea?'

'Well, I know she died when Gina was very young, but—'

'And before she died she was useless. Lost interest in the poor kid after it happened. Isn't that right, darling?'

'I—don't remember,' she said unsteadily.

'Well, I do. My mum got really mad on your behalf. Said she couldn't understand how any mother—'

'Excuse me,' Gina said hurriedly, and fled the room.

She hardly knew where she was going. Tears blurred her eyes, and she felt as though she'd been slashed with knives. How could Dan have said something so insensitive, when he must realise how painful those memories were for her?

But of course, he didn't realise. Dan never understood how anybody felt about anything.

With a huge effort she pulled herself together. Dan had followed her, puzzled and hearty.

'What's up, darling? Not like you to throw a wobbly.'

'No, I'm so reliable, aren't I?' she said with a touch of bitterness.

'Pardon?'

'Nothing. I'm just tired. Thank you for a lovely evening, Dan.'

'Wasn't bad, was it? Better than all that fancy stuff.'

'A plain man,' Carson said from behind him. 'A man after my own heart. You and I must get together some time soon and discuss that new plug you were telling me about—'

As he spoke he was guiding Dan remorselessly to the door. Dan never knew quite how he found himself outside without claiming a goodnight kiss from Gina. But before he could protest the front door was closed.

Carson returned to the kitchen, where Gina was now washing up the coffee cups.

'Leave that,' he told her.

'No trouble. I like things to be tidy before I go to bed,' she said brightly.

'I said leave it. Let's talk.'

'Nothing to talk about.'

'After *that*, there's nothing to talk about?' he demanded in outrage.

'If you mean that I deceived you—I'm sorry.'

'Deceived me?'

'I suppose I rather gave the impression that my mother was perfect—and that's how I knew what Joey needed—'

'The hell with that! Gina, will you put those things away?'

'Yes, I've finished now. I'm going to bed.'

'Not yet. Let me pour you a brandy. You look as if you've had a nasty shock.'

'I'm fine, honestly.'

He took hold of her arms. 'Then why are you trembling?'

'I'm not—I'm just tired—'

She would have run away but he was still holding her firmly. The feel of his hands on her bare skin was unnerving, but not as unnerving as the gentleness with which he said, 'Tell me about it, Gina.'

'There's nothing to tell,' she said desperately. 'She's dead. It was all a long time ago—'

He let his hands fall. 'I see,' he said in a hard voice.

Something in it alerted her. 'What do you see?'

'It's all right for you to listen to my problems, but when I ask about yours it's stand-off time.'

'No, it isn't like that—'

'You've seen things about my life that I've shown to nobody else. It's not nice to be kept at a distance after that. In fact, it's pretty patronising.'

'I'm not—'

'I'm supposed to trust you, but you don't trust me. I thought we were friends. If I didn't think that I wouldn't have confided in you as much as I have. Apparently it's all one-way.' He spoke sharply to conceal the hurt that had taken him by surprise.

Her voice shook. 'There's really nothing to tell. Nothing at all. Now I'm going to bed.'

She wrenched herself free and almost ran up the stairs to get away from him. Carson watched her go, bitterly, wondering what had come over him in the last few minutes.

Be damned to her! What right did she have to insinuate herself into Joey's heart, then go off and marry that oaf? If that was all the taste she had...!

He poured himself a large whisky. He needed it.

The house had been transformed since she'd filled it with her laughter and warmth. And now she planned to vanish, leaving an emptiness behind that he—that *Joey*—would find painful. It had been bearable before she came, but it wouldn't be bearable now. Better never to have known her than suffer like this.

He had a pile of work to do. For an hour he tried to settle to it, but she'd destroyed his concentration. Another black mark against her! The sooner she left the better. Then they would all know where they stood.

At last Carson gave up the pretence of working. His head was aching again from an evening that had been an unexpected strain. He didn't bother to turn on the hall light, but climbed the stairs in the darkness. On the top step he nearly stumbled over something.

'Gina, what are you doing sitting on the stairs?'

'I don't know.' She gave a sniff and blew her nose. 'I was going to come down for a drink, then I changed my mind. At least, I nearly did. Then I wasn't sure. So I sat down while I decided. That was ten minutes ago— I think.'

'You're babbling,' he said kindly.

'Yes, I suppose I am.'

He sat down beside her. In the poor light from the landing window he could just see that she'd taken off the lovely dress and put on a cheap cotton dressing gown. It was lucky she was used to counting her blessings, he thought, in a kind of rage, because when she'd married Dan she'd be wearing cheap dressing gowns for the rest of her life.

Then she sniffed again and his rage died. 'Have you been crying?'

'If I said no, would you believe me?'

'No.'

'Then I have.'

'Because of me? Because I was unkind to you? I'm sorry for those things I said.'

'No, it's not you. It's—it's everything.'

'Dan, dragging your unhappy memories into the light?'

'Mmm!'

'He shouldn't have done that. It was insensitive of him.'

'Oh, Dan's all right. He means well, but he just says the first thing that comes into his head.'

'Even if it hurts people?'

'Well, I suppose I'm making too much of it. It was a long time ago.'

'But she was your mother.'

'Yes, she was,' Gina said huskily. 'And I didn't understand why she suddenly couldn't bear to look at me. I was ill, and when I got better I was deaf, and it was like I'd changed into a different person. I kept thinking, one day I'd get it right, and she'd be pleased. Only, then she died—'

She'd been trying not to cry, but suddenly the grief of years overwhelmed her and she dropped her head and sobbed, an inconsolable child again. Carson slipped an arm around her shoulders, and felt them heave. Somewhere deep inside him he was cursing, though whether he was cursing Dan, Gina's mother, Joey's mother, or simply himself for being so useless to comfort her, he didn't know. He only knew that she was unhappy, and somebody ought to be made to pay.

He drew her against him, putting his other arm around her, so that her head fitted against his shoulder, and he rested his cheek against it.

'I'll never get it right now,' Gina choked. 'My last memories of her are all of how angry she used to get because I couldn't work out what she wanted. She used to shout at me—I couldn't hear but I knew she was shouting by the way she tensed up—and there was a terrible hostile look in her eyes, as though I were being stupid on purpose. If people came, she told me to stay out of sight—'

'Dear God!' Carson said with soft violence.

'One day, when I was ten, she got terribly impatient. And the more impatient she was, the more I got it wrong. In the end she stormed out of the house. I felt so wicked, but I didn't know what I'd done. I sat on the stairs, making plans about how it would be when she came back—how we'd try again, and I'd get it right this time.

'But she never came back. She collided with a lorry and was killed outright. I thought it was my fault.'

Carson tightened his arms about her, beyond speech.

'I haven't remembered all this for years,' she said at last. 'It was there, but I wouldn't look at it. And when my father didn't cope very well either I suppose I balanced that by building her up in my mind. You can tell yourself all sorts of comforting lies about people who aren't there.'

He rested his cheek against her hair. 'Yes,' he murmured, half to himself. 'That's true enough.'

Gina sighed. 'It wasn't really her fault. I think she was a light-hearted person who enjoyed a good time. When things didn't turn out that way, it threw her.'

'Thousands of mothers cope,' Carson said, angry for her again. 'Why must you let her off the hook?'

'Maybe because it hurts less that way.' She made a valiant effort to pull herself together. 'I'm all right,' she said huskily, dabbing her eyes. 'I don't know what came over me to act like that.'

'Some wounds don't heal,' Carson said. 'And if we try to pretend they have that only makes it worse, somehow.'

'Yes,' she whispered, thinking of the woman who had left him wounded and unable to heal.

'You've been strong for Joey, and for me,' Carson went on. 'But who's strong for you?'

'There have been people who've helped. Mrs Braith, Dan's mother, who taught me signing. She was kind, and he used to look after me a lot when we were children.'

Carson's eyes hardened at the thought of Dan, her chosen husband, who would let her down again and again. He enfolded her more closely in his arms, wishing he knew what to say. But did he show up any better than the people who'd failed her? Wasn't that failure exactly what she had recognised in him?

Then he felt her arms creeping around him, as though she found a kind of comfort in the warmth of his body. He stroked her hair, feeling how slight she was against his powerful frame. It was her spirit that was strong.

Tough, she'd said, only a short time ago. But it was the wrong word. She had the strength of finely spun tensile steel, but she could be hurt and broken with a word.

'I guess you've got a good deal to cry about,' he said.

'Oh, I don't cry any more—well, not really. I got all that over years ago.'

He lifted her chin and brushed a tear from her cheek. 'Is that so? Now you just dry other people's tears.'

She managed a tremulous smile, and Carson drew a sharp breath at the sight.

'It's all right,' he said softly. 'Everything's going to be all right.' He didn't know what the words meant, only that he had to say something.

Gina heard him, not just in her ears but in her bones. Every part of her seemed to respond to that assurance of comfort and safety. She wanted to remain enfolded in his arms like this for ever, enjoying the sweet warmth creeping through her, until there was nothing else.

Carson stayed looking down into her face, feeling as though he was held in a dream. It was the night of her engagement to another man, and he had no right to kiss her. But while his conscience was arguing his lips were pressing themselves against hers.

Her mouth was wide and curved, generous to match her heart, and somehow just the right shape for his own mouth. It had been winter in his life for so long that the coming of spring was a shock, making his blood sing and his rational mind take a holiday.

For Gina, with only Dan for comparison, Carson's kiss came as a revelation. She hadn't known that a man's lips could be so subtle, so skilful, or that it was possible to be so completely lost in sensation. His mouth was gentle, teasing her from one caress to another, so that she responded without thinking.

She'd yearned for this since the night he fell asleep on the sofa and she'd looked longingly at his mouth. It was forbidden fruit, and all the sweeter for it. This was why she couldn't let Dan kiss her again.

She no longer had any power of thought, or even any desire to think. She wanted this, and every passing moment, every movement of his lips, made her want it more. She wanted other things, too, things to do with the feeling of danger at the thinness of her nightdress and her nakedness beneath.

She was trembling with the awakening of new life. His lips were thrilling but they weren't enough. She desired his hands too, and his whole body pressed against hers, uniting with hers.

She slipped her arm about his neck and drew him closer, inviting him to explore her more intimately. Somehow his tongue was in her mouth, setting off sensations that were intense and glorious. She gave herself up to them joyfully, aching for the intimacy of his touch, her heart beating wildly. She felt his arms tighten about her and the power flowing from his body to hers.

Wherever his tongue flicked against the inside of her mouth, it set off new flares of feeling. She hadn't known that a man's touch could make a woman feel like that, as though she would do anything—break any rule—to make him hers.

She melted against him, letting his arms support her while her hands discovered the strong column of his neck, the breadth of his chest. She felt giddy, lying there in the darkness, barely able to see him, but feeling him with every part of her.

It was like the time she'd knelt beside him on the sofa, and his breath had brushed her mouth. She was so alive to Carson that he had only to touch her in one place to touch her everywhere. The electric sensation of his mouth against hers was reflected over her skin, her breasts, her loins.

Carson was too experienced a lover not to sense that Gina was on the verge of total surrender. His pulses leapt and his kisses grew deeper, more urgent and intense. In a moment he would carry her to bed, and she would let him because his skilled caresses had overcome her will.

To hell with Dan! A man had no right to a woman if he couldn't keep her.

But the thought of Dan was fatal. To Carson he might seem an oaf, but to Gina he was the man she'd chosen—heaven alone knew why!

The struggle with himself was terrible, but he won. Gina had brought him priceless gifts, and he couldn't repay her by overcoming her when she was at her most vulnerable.

Gina could feel his breath coming harshly, sense his heart beating strongly. His arms were relaxing their hold; he was drawing away. Now she was eager to see his face and find in it some reflection of her own joy.

But when she saw it her heart sank. It was full of caution and dismay, like that of a man who was asking himself how he could have been so stupid. A chill ran through her.

'Perhaps that wasn't a good idea,' he said unsteadily. 'I wouldn't like you to think—I wanted to make you feel better, but I guess I chose the wrong way.'

Gina tried to collect her scattered thoughts. Through the singing in her blood she was vaguely aware that Carson was uttering words that denied what had just happened between them. But he couldn't be. It was too beautiful and poignant to be denied.

He was disengaging himself. 'Please don't worry, Gina. I know you're very vulnerable in this house, and I won't be forcing myself on you.'

'Carson, I don't—'

'After all, I understand how things are between you and Dan—I just don't want you to be worried.'

'I'm not,' she said in a colourless voice. 'You were just trying to make me feel better.'

'Yes,' he said quickly. 'That was it. I went a little too far. Don't hold it against me, for Joey's sake.'

'Of course not.' To her own surprise her voice came out sounding normal. 'I—I think I'd better go to bed now.'

'Yes,' he said hastily. 'Me too.'

How anxious he was to get away from her! she thought sadly. How stupid the dreams of a moment ago seemed now! She bid him a hasty goodnight and fled to her room.

CHAPTER EIGHT

AT BREAKFAST next morning Carson said, without looking at her, 'I'll be home early tonight to let you go out.'

'Go out? I'm not going anywhere,' Gina said, puzzled.

'Aren't you meeting Dan to buy the engagement ring?'

'Enga—?' She rose from the table, full of wrath. 'What has Dan been saying to you?'

'Last night he said—well, he implied—' The glint in her eyes was thrilling, if a little unnerving, and her hair glowed redder than ever. 'He implied he'd asked you to marry him and—'

'Yes, he asked me, but I didn't answer because I couldn't get his attention away from the race. You mean he just took it for granted, *and he told you*—?' She took a long breath. 'If Dan was here this minute I'd—well, it's lucky for him that he isn't.'

'You're not going to marry him?'

'Not in a million years,' she said emphatically. 'I'd have told you—how could you think? *Oh-h-h* I could—'

A lock of fiery hair fell over her brow. She pushed it back. Carson watched her with delight. The sun had come out again.

As he went to the front door Joey joined him, anxiously signing. *Are you and Gina cross?*

'No,' Carson told him. 'In fact, things couldn't be better.'

When her temper had calmed, Gina called Dan.

'I blame myself,' she said. 'I should have told you

115

last night that I couldn't marry you, but there was so much going on.'

'But we had it all settled.'

'Dan, we didn't settle anything. We barely mentioned marriage between races. That's no way to decide something so important.'

'Gina, we've known for ages that we were going to get married. We haven't made a fuss about it, but it's been taken for granted.'

'Maybe that's why we shouldn't. We've been good friends. Let's keep it that way.'

He argued for a while, but she knew there was no going back. When Dan hung up he sounded bewildered rather than heartbroken. He would find someone else, she thought, someone who would appreciate the qualities he had and not worry about the ones he hadn't. Once, that girl might have been herself, but now it was as though she'd been overtaken by a kind of divine discontent.

Carson seemed to be there with her, touching her face with gentle fingers, regarding her mouth with pleasure, kissing it so tenderly and lovingly that her heart almost stopped from the beauty of it. And then drawing back. Why? Because he thought she was engaged to Dan? Yes, she thought excitedly, because of that.

Only that? Was she fooling herself with what she longed to believe?

Dan had said, 'You'd never even think of him in that way.' But the thought had been lurking there since the first day, when Carson had sat in Bob's Café and made the surroundings look drab against his vivid life. He'd disturbed her, but she'd thought that was because of the car incident. The truth was that he disturbed her because he disturbed her. There was no other reason.

She became aware that Joey was trying to get her attention, puzzled, because it was the first time she'd ever been oblivious to his needs.

Why are you smiling like that?

She hadn't known she was smiling. 'Because I'm happy.'

Why?

'It would take too long to tell you. Let's go out for a drive.'

In the peanut?

'If you like.'

Carson had placed a smart, expensive car at her disposal, but Joey's preferred method of transport was the peanut, and the other car stood, ignored and unloved, in the garage.

They went to a nearby aquadrome, and spent the day boating.

Arriving home in the evening, Gina found a message on the answering machine to say that Carson would be late after all. On the whole he kept his promise to be early, but sometimes a delay couldn't be helped.

Joey was worn out from his day, and almost fell asleep over his tea, so Gina didn't anticipate trouble at bedtime.

She was wrong.

Joey wanted to stay up to see his father. There followed an argument conducted with furiously flashing fingers, in which Gina tried to convince Joey that 'bedtime' meant 'bedtime'. He could fight his corner as stubbornly as any other child, and after a while he gave up on fingers and settled for shaking his head. Whereupon Gina also gave up on fingers, tossed him over her shoulder and marched upstairs.

She came down half an hour later, worn out but smiling. She poured herself a glass of wine and settled down for an evening with the television. But none of the programmes appealed to her, and she began to rummage among Carson's collection of videos.

Some were shop-bought, many were business programmes taped from television. At last Gina came to one which had no label or anything to indicate what it might be. Intrigued, she put it on.

She found herself looking at a churchyard on a bright summer's day. The church was a beautiful old ivy-clad building made of grey stone, with a tower and a steeple. And there, coming through the porch, was a bride and groom.

The bride was dazzlingly lovely in a flowing white dress and veil. Everything about her was perfect—her face, her figure, her hair, the gaze she turned on the young man beside her. And his eyes never left her. For him she was the only woman on earth.

Then Gina realised she was looking at Carson.

This was the wedding of the young Carson Page and Brenda, the girl who'd gone on to become Angelica Duvaine. Barely conscious of her own actions, Gina sat up and leaned forward, alert to every nuance as the young bride and groom came more clearly into view.

Here was Carson as she had never dreamed he could look: a young man with all the hope and joy of life before him, brilliantly, whole-heartedly in love.

It was there in his eyes as he gazed down adoringly at his bride—surely the loveliest bride any groom had been blessed with. They walked out of the church into the sunlight, sure that the sunlight would last for ever.

The cameraman tracked them as they came down the path, laughing and ducking confetti. Then they got into the black limousine, where his arm immediately went around her, drawing her close for a kiss that threatened the ruin of her veil. As they drove off they were oblivious of the crowds. They needed only each other.

A curious little pain had started in Gina's breast. She wanted to turn the video off and wipe out those glorious young people whose love excluded everyone else. She longed to obliterate that handsome young man who'd thought he had all he could ever want, and nothing could hurt him. Above all, she didn't want to see the adoration with which he looked at the woman.

She wanted to switch off, but she couldn't move. She had to watch as the scene moved to the reception. How proudly he escorted his bride to the top table, how tenderly he pulled out a chair for her, and bestowed a quick kiss on her before standing up, then leaned down for another. He kissed her whenever he could.

Now the speeches. 'On behalf of my wife and myself...' Cheers and laughter. Carson looked self-conscious and very young. He couldn't have been more than twenty-five, so confident and happy, so different from the bitter, tense man he'd become.

The pictures flickered out, then started up again, a few months later. There was Brenda, heavily pregnant, still managing to look glamorous. They were in a garden and Carson was leading her towards a seat, adjusting the cushions, holding her hand, regarding her tenderly, bursting with pride. The pictures faded again.

More pictures. Brenda sitting up in bed, her newborn baby in her arms, a doting expression on her face, yet still managing to pose so that she was seen to best advantage. Even in hospital she was perfectly made up and there was calculation in her every movement. Gina could see it clearly now. She wondered how long it had been before Carson saw it.

There was Carson with his little son in his arms. The boy had grown; he might be a year old. Carson was holding him high in the air, smiling into his eyes, the picture of fatherly pride. The child too looked happy, his face covered in a fat, gleeful baby grin as he gazed down fearlessly at the man whose big hands held him high and safe.

Gently the father lowered his child, settling him on his arm so that they could look at each other. Gina watched, transfixed. The picture was enchanting in itself, but full of heartache to anyone who knew what had come after.

A noise made her turn her head. Joey was standing there, his eyes fixed on the screen. Gina reached out and touched him, drawing him to the sofa to sit beside her.

Have you ever seen this before? she signed.

He shook his head.

'Do you know who that is?'

Daddy—a long pause—*and me.*

Now a close-up, showing the pride and joy in Carson's face as he regarded his son. Joey never moved. His eyes were fixed on his father with a yearning expression that brought tears to Gina's eyes. What was the child thinking? That he never saw such a look from his father these days?

The screen went dark.

'That's it, darling.' She gave him a hug. 'Bedtime.'

But Joey shook his head. *Again.*

Gina hesitated, wondering if this was good for him. But he turned beseeching eyes on her, and she knew she couldn't refuse him. She rewound to the start of the scene. Joey watched, riveted, a little smile on his face.

Again.

'Just once more,' she told him. 'Then bed.'

Joey took the handset and, to her dismay, wound the tape right back to the start so that the wedding came up again. Gina wished time itself could be rewound, so that she could go back to the point where she was rummaging through the videos. Then she would put that one aside, and never have to see Carson's face as he looked at the love of his life.

She didn't doubt that was what Brenda was, because no man ever looked like that at more than one woman. Besides, he'd told her on the night he'd confided about his marriage, 'I had some very naive notions in those days—true love conquers all… If ever a man and woman loved each other, we did. And it all fell apart like a shoddy toy.'

Brenda had used up all his capacity to love, leaving behind only a husk. Now she knew why he'd drawn back from the kiss that meant so much to her. It wasn't because of Dan. It was because he was a fair man, and wouldn't risk making her love him when he had no heart to give. Why, he'd practically warned her!

She closed her eyes, longing to escape the racking jealousy that would overwhelm her if she had to see him gaze at his bride. But it was no use; he was there behind her eyelids. And so was Brenda, her lovely face seeming to say that what was hers was hers for ever, even when she no longer wanted it.

Carson was a prickly, difficult man who went at life like a bull at a gate, and hurt himself more often than anyone else. He expected everything to be as straightforward as a business deal and, when it wasn't, he was lost. But beneath the rough exterior he was sensitive and easily hurt. He'd reached out to her in his awkward way, and gained a hold on her heart that was painful and unbreakable.

He needed her, at least for the moment. Perhaps, for Joey's sake, he might even come to feel a kind of affection for her. But he wouldn't gaze at her with the passionate adoration he'd offered Brenda.

And that was what she wanted, more than she'd ever wanted anything in her whole life. In the years when she'd longed to hear again, she'd thought that was wanting. But it had been nothing like the yearning that possessed her now, for something she could never have.

As the wedding scenes began again she heard Carson's key in the lock and went to meet him with relief.

'What's the matter?' he asked, seeing her anxious face.

'I was watching some of your tapes and I found one that seems to be home movies,' she said, speaking quickly. 'There are some pictures of you with Joey when he was a baby, and he came in while I was playing them. Carson, please go carefully. It makes him so happy to see them—I don't want anything to spoil it for him.' She saw him frown and added quickly, 'I suppose I shouldn't have been looking at your private video—'

'Never mind. I should have put it away, but I forgot it was there.'

Together they moved quietly into the doorway, and Gina heard Carson's swift intake of breath. Joey was looking at his mother, smiling at her baby.

The little boy looked up and saw them. He touched the place behind his ear that was almost healed now, and signed something.

'What did he say?' Carson asked hoarsely.

Gina spoke with difficulty. 'He asked—if his mother would come back—when he can hear again.'

She tried to give the child some kind of answer, to

say that Brenda hadn't gone away because of his deafness. But he gazed at her with sad, wise eyes until she gave up. After that he didn't ask any more.

He watched the scene again, then again. Finally he froze a frame showing Brenda dropping a kiss on the forehead of the child that lay in her arms. And he sat there, gazing at it.

Gina turned away and went hurriedly into the kitchen. After a moment Carson followed her.

'My God!' he said softly. 'My God!'

'That poor little boy,' Gina said huskily.

'All this time I've tried to tell myself that Joey understood—about why I've tried to keep his mother away—I didn't know he felt that way about her. Maybe I didn't give him the chance to tell me.'

'I do my best for him, but I can't touch his real pain,' Gina said with a sigh. 'She's his mother.'

'A terrible mother—'

'But still, his mother. And he wants her.'

'He wants a fiction created out of his own imagination. The reality would only break his heart again.'

'That picture of her holding him wasn't imagination. It was real.'

'But it stopped being real the moment she discovered that he had problems with his hearing. Why can't he face it?'

'Because he's not quite eight years old. How can you expect him to face the fact that his mother doesn't love him?'

'Especially when his father's such a miserable failure,' Carson growled. 'I suppose he had to cling onto something when I let him down too, and it was easier to fantasise about her, because she isn't here.' His eyes met hers. 'You know all about that.'

'Yes, I do. But don't knock yourself. At least you're trying now.'

'Perhaps if I talked to him—I can do that now—try to explain that she—that—'

'Can you explain why she never writes to him, never so much as sends him an email? She could do that easily enough, if she'd only bother.'

'I thought she did. I'm sure they email each other.'

'Yes, I thought so, until I read some of hers. She doesn't write them, Carson. They read like a press release. I'm sure her secretary is very efficient.'

'Damn her!' he breathed.

'Please, go and say something to him now.'

To their relief Joey was no longer looking at his mother. He'd returned to the pictures of himself and his father. As Carson came in he looked up and signed something.

'Is that me?' Gina translated, seeing that Carson was having trouble.

He put himself where Joey could see. 'Yes, that's you,' he said slowly. 'You were a great kid and—and you still are.'

The brilliant happiness in his son's smile shocked him. Such a small compliment, but it meant the world to a child who wasn't used to being told he was valued.

Joey pointed to the screen, and his fingers worked fast.

'Where—?' Carson concentrated hard. 'Where was— Mummy? Mummy was taking our picture.'

More signing.

'I don't understand,' Carson said urgently to Gina.

'He said, "Were we all happy?"'

A strange, withered look came over Carson's face. 'Yes,' he said at last. 'Yes, we were happy.'

Before Joey could ask another question Gina tapped him on the shoulder and signed, *Hungry?*

Luckily this diverted him and he scrambled off the sofa and into the kitchen. Carson secured the video and put it away before following Joey and settling down to talk to him, while Gina put some pizza in the oven.

She deliberately stayed in the background until the snack was over and they put Joey back to bed together. The child was happy now, unaware that his very happiness was turning a knife in his father's heart.

When they had left the room and closed the door Carson said, 'Los Angeles is eight hours behind us. I might get her.'

He went down to his office and dialled his ex-wife's number. Gina didn't try to listen, but she couldn't help hearing Carson saying, with edgy patience, 'Just get her to the phone. I'll wait.'

It was a long wait. Gina took him coffee and he gave her a brief smile.

'She's a star, and they never come to the phone at once,' he said wryly.

But at last it seemed that Brenda had kept him waiting as long as she felt her status demanded, and Gina heard him say, 'Brenda—what are you—? Never mind that. I need to talk to you seriously.'

Gina slipped out of earshot, although she longed to hear what Carson said.

She busied herself about the kitchen, finding things to do, trying not to think of what might be being said in Carson's study, and why it was taking so long.

He would be trying to make Brenda see that her place was with her son. They might even have a reconciliation. That would be the best thing for Joey. That was what she wanted.

Or, at least, she might make herself want it, if she tried hard enough.

But when Carson returned his face told a story of defeat.

'She says she's about to start some TV show, and she hasn't time to visit him,' he said bitterly. 'She also reminded me of the efforts I'd made to keep them apart, which I suppose I deserved. I suggested taking Joey out there to see her, and she nearly had hysterics. Nobody knows she has a deaf son, and nobody must know. Some mother!'

'Did you tell her about the operation?'

'I tried. But Brenda listens to about one word in ten. I got halfway before she broke in, "Do you mean he's cured now?" I tried to explain that it isn't a cure, and even when he can hear something he's still going to need time and a lot of help before he can talk. When she discovered that nobody had waved a magic wand she lost interest.'

'But even if one parent is lost to him, he still has the other. You can be the best father there's ever been, and the happier he is with you, the less he'll miss her. And I'm here to help.'

He closed his eyes suddenly, just as he'd done at their first meeting.

'Show me the way, Gina,' he said softly. 'This is the most important thing in the world, and I can't do it without you.'

His weariness touched her heart. She wanted to reach out and enfold him in her arms, promise to make everything right for him. But she knew if she did that she would try to make him kiss her again, and she didn't dare. She wasn't sure where she stood with him, or what he really wanted.

But once the thought had come to her she couldn't keep her eyes from his mouth, so that she seemed to feel it on hers again, as it had been only last night. Surely he remembered how it had been? What was to stop him kissing her again?

'Gina,' he said uncertainly.

'Yes?'

'I'm sorry I was late getting home tonight. I know I promised.'

'It's all right,' she said, trying to hide her disappointment. 'But time is passing and soon he'll be back at school. You promised him a holiday.'

'Can we still take it—as he is?'

'He can't fly or go swimming, but if we stick to our original plan he'll be all right.'

'Then next week I'm clearing my desk, and we'll go.'

'That's marvellous. Joey will be so thrilled.'

'I'll have to leave the planning to you—to you and Joey. Arrange whatever he wants, even if it means visiting every aquarium in the country.'

'Oh, no,' she said seriously. 'Only one or two come up to his standards. But he'll tell you all about that.'

CHAPTER NINE

THEY set their departure for nine o'clock next Monday morning. Gina was glancing around her room to see if she'd forgotten anything, when Carson looked in.

'Ready to go?'

'All present and correct,' she said cheerfully.

She opened the connecting door to Joey's room, and stopped at what she saw there. Alerted by her sudden stillness, Carson came and stood beside her.

Joey, oblivious to them, was standing before his mother's picture. His hands moved as he explained to her that he was going away, but would come back soon. When he'd finished, he stepped back and made his final gesture, hands folded, crossed at the wrists and laid against his chest.

'What does that mean?' Carson asked quietly.

'It's the sign for love,' Gina said heavily. 'He's saying that he loves her.'

'Damn her! *Damn her!*'

Gina forced herself to smile as she went in and attracted Joey's attention. He took her hand eagerly and almost pulled her downstairs. Once outside, he couldn't resist displaying his quirky sense of humour by heading for Gina's little car.

Carson touched him on the shoulder and spoke. Now that he addressed Joey more often, the little boy was growing skilled at reading his lips. 'This way.'

But aren't we going in the peanut?

A vision of three people and four suitcases being

squashed into the tiny vehicle made Carson grin and Gina chuckle. Joey hiccuped with laughter as she ruffled his hair.

'You shouldn't call it a peanut,' Carson told him. 'It isn't polite.'

You did.

'Well, I'll be— Who told you that?'

Gina. She said you called it a peanut on wheels.

'Oh, did she? Well, you're a cheeky little wretch!'

It was delightful to see Carson sharing the joke with his son.

And what is Gina?

'What is Gina? Well, Gina is—'

She waited, her heart beating unreasonably fast.

'I don't know,' Carson said at last. 'What shall we call Gina? You say.'

For answer Joey raised one hand, the fingers together, the thumb apart. He rested the thumb briefly against the side of his face, drew it away, returned it, then away again.

Gina felt as though something was choking her. Joey had made the sign for 'mother'.

'We should be going,' she said hastily. 'Or we'll get caught up in traffic.'

It was three hundred miles to the little coastal resort of Kenningham. Once it had been packed every summer, then its popularity had declined. But it had fought back with a funfair, and a first-class aquarium, and now it was flourishing again.

'You did book us in somewhere, didn't you?' Carson asked as they drove along the crowded seafront.

'At the Grand, with rooms overlooking the sea.'

She'd booked two rooms—one for Carson and one for

herself and Joey. As they unpacked Joey was in a fever of excitement, like any child at the seaside.

When can we go to the aquarium?

'Soon.'

Now?

'Not now. Your father has driven a long way. He's tired and he needs a meal.'

After that?

'As soon as we can.'

But today, today, today!

She looked at her watch. 'I don't know when the aquarium closes.'

Then can't we go now?

And so they came back to the beginning of the argument.

It was a first-class hotel with an haute cuisine restaurant, but Carson, who was learning fast about his son, declined this in favour of a nearby burger place.

'I think I deserve a medal for getting it right this time,' he joked, watching Joey stuff himself with burger and chips.

'Yes,' she agreed. 'And it's quicker eating here, so maybe we'll get into the aquarium before it closes.'

'We will. I've checked closing time, and we have another three hours.' He saw her admiringly raised eyebrows, and said self-consciously, 'Organisation. That's the key to a successful enterprise.'

'I'm impressed. Why don't you tell Joey?'

Joey was eating with one hand and holding a brightly coloured pamphlet in the other. He showed it to them, pointing to something in the small print. They looked at each other and laughed.

The pamphlet was about the aquarium and Joey had found the opening times.

'He's not your son for nothing,' she said. 'He must have picked that up in the hotel foyer. Now that's real organisation.'

'Yes, it is.' Carson regarded his offspring fondly.

'Why don't you ask him now to tell you about wrasse?' she suggested, adding quickly, 'You haven't cheated, have you?'

'No, I don't even know how the word is spelled.'

She spelled it for him and Carson turned to Joey.

'What can you tell me about wrasse?'

Joey looked quizzical, as though unsure how seriously to take this request.

'Go on. Tell me.'

Joey needed no more encouragement. He began signing and spelling so vigorously that Carson had to stop him.

'Steady,' he said, speaking. 'You go too fast for me.'

Joey nodded and went back to the beginning. Carson watched his fingers, his brow furrowed with concentration.

'Wait,' he said at last. 'Do it again. I couldn't understand—I thought you said—no, that must be wrong.'

Joey shook his head. *Not misunderstand.*

'Go on,' Gina urged. 'Make it easy for your father.'

'Thanks,' Carson said with a grin.

Joey did it all again while Carson watched his fingers and his frown grew deeper.

'You're kidding me!' he said explosively at last, forgetting to sign or speak slowly. But Joey understood and grinned.

'Did I get that right?' Carson demanded of Gina.

'It is pretty incredible, isn't it?'

'He says wrasse is a fish. And they're all female— that is, they're all *born* female.'

'Good. Go on.'

'They live in groups of about twenty females to one male, and when the male dies one of the females changes sex, and becomes the resident male? You expect me to believe that?'

'Don't ask me. Joey's the expert.'

He turned to his son, looking harassed. 'That can't be true.'

Joey nodded, then finger-spelled, *Aquarium—wait*.

After that Carson was as eager as his son to get going, because he wanted to find out if he was being taken for a ride.

As soon as they were inside the aquarium it was obvious that Joey was different from other children. Instead of lingering over the more colourful or outrageous creatures, he bypassed them, to spend long periods studying small fish and shells which to the untrained eye looked drab and uninteresting.

'He's like a little professor,' Carson said.

'Yes, he is. When he's on his own subject he's older than his years.'

Joey passed from one esoteric item to another, deeply absorbed, leaving the other two to pass the time with the more accessible exhibits.

'I feel like I'm the child and he's the adult,' Carson complained, although not too seriously. 'Joey.' He tapped the boy on the shoulder but Joey, instead of turning, held up a hand, flapping it slightly in a gesture that clearly said, Not now. I'm busy.

'Did you see that?' Carson demanded.

'Don't get mad at him.'

'I'm not mad. I'm just wondering what's happening here.'

'It's simple. You're in the presence of a superior intellect.'

'I'm beginning to believe you.' He sounded dazed.

Joey came out of his happy trance, smiling at them.

'Wrasse,' Carson said firmly.

Joey nodded like a teacher telling his class that the time had come, and beckoned them to follow him.

And there it was, wrasse, with a notice beside the tank, confirming everything Joey had said. Carson was speechless. Joey regarded his father with his head on one side as if to say, Believe me, huh?

Carson's answer delighted Gina. He extended his hand. Joey placed his small child's hand in it, and they shook, man to man.

There wasn't time to see everything, but Joey was ready to leave, on the promise of a return visit next day. They paused in the bookshop long enough for Carson to load him up with enough literature to keep him happy for the evening. He also purchased a basic introduction to the subject for himself—a survival mechanism, he explained to Gina.

They had a merry evening. Joey was allowed to stay up late because it was a holiday, and by the time he was ready for bed the other two were feeling glad of an early night.

Another visit to the aquarium was the first thing on the next day's agenda. Gina and Carson might feel that they'd seen everything, but the expert had barely started.

But at last he took pity on them, seeming to understand that not everyone could be riveted by a mollusc the size of a penny. They headed downstairs to where they could walk through the aquarium's main attraction, a huge perspex tunnel through the water. Sharks swam beside them, flatfish drifted overhead, and lobsters scuttled beneath their feet. Joey pointed out what neither of them had noticed—a conger eel peering from its hiding place, motionless, cold-eyed and evil.

Over burgers and orange squash it was agreed that the adults needed a little light relief, and they headed for the funfair. Here Joey stopped being a professor and became an excited little boy, darting hither and thither, wanting to try everything at once. A go on the rifle range showed that he had a keen, straight eye. Not to be outdone, Carson also took a turn, but managed only one bull's-eye to Joey's three.

A contest ensued, at the end of which Gina was laden down with furry toys and plastic jewellery, and her two escorts were thoroughly pleased with themselves and each other.

At last Joey stopped in front of the Ghost Train. Skulls leered, skeletons dangled, hideous creatures darted and peeped. It was the most effectively horrible Ghost Train that Gina had ever seen. Joey gave a sigh of pure pleasure.

'This?' Gina asked him.

He nodded vigorously.

'You're sure?' she said faintly.

He nodded again.

'I don't think we have a choice,' Carson said.

He paid three entrance fees and they squeezed into a car, Joey on the inside, Gina in the middle and Carson on the outside.

'I don't like these things,' Gina said. 'I never did.'

'But you have both of us to look after you,' Carson pointed out mischievously.

A hideous wailing drowned him out. With a jolt the cars began to move, pushing through the black curtains ahead of them. Then they were inside, swerving violently from side to side, the ghastly moaning louder, sounding as though it was everywhere.

Neon skeletons appeared and vanished. Gruesome figures loomed and leered. Gina glanced down at Joey, but she needn't have worried. The flickering lights showed that he was relishing every moment.

She wished she could say the same of herself. Of course her rational mind knew that it was only paint, cardboard and a few special effects. But her irrational side flinched from the things that swooped out of the darkness without warning. Something flapped in her face, making her jump and squeal.

'Are you all right?' Carson asked, slipping a protective arm about her.

She had to make him repeat it, as the noise was playing havoc with her implant. Understanding, he said it clearly in a brief interlude of bilious green light, and this time she managed to follow his lips.

'Of course I'm all right,' she said, trying for dignity. But the effect was ruined by a huge grinning skull that appeared in front of them, getting bigger and bigger—

Then the car charged right through it and the darkness enfolded them again.

'Yuck!'

Carson's arm tightened. At the same time she felt his fingers gently on her chin, urging her head to look at him.

'As long as you don't turn into a skull,' she pleaded.

Crimson light came and went, casting his eyes into shadows and giving him a satanic look. It crossed her mind that if she were skilled in the traditional female arts she might use this situation. She could do a little swooning and screaming, then cast herself on Carson's manly chest for protection, and the rest would follow. Maybe Victorian maidens knew a thing or two after all.

But she'd been reared in a different school, and for the life of her she couldn't have put on such a performance.

Then help came in the form of a freezing skeleton that swooped down from the roof and caressed her face, before vanishing. Startled, Gina gave a perfectly genuine shriek and the next moment her face was buried against Carson's shoulder. She could feel him shaking with laughter.

'Beast!' she said in a muffled voice.

Through a break in the moaning she heard him say, 'It's all right, it's gone now.'

'I'm not looking up. That thing was *disgusting*!'

'It's safe, I promise you.'

Tentatively she raised her eyes and found that they were in total darkness. The hellish moans had resumed, but there were no more flashing lights. She waited, ready to duck again if anything touched her face.

But when she felt the first soft brush against her lips she didn't duck. Nor did she want to turn away from what might be happening. Rather, she wanted to stay and make sure that it really *was* happening.

It was the lightest of feather touches, a soft caress of lips on lips, now here, now gone. Perhaps real, perhaps imagined. In the darkness she couldn't be sure.

But then it came again, a little firmer this time, a lot more determined. Warm lips moving over hers, asking silent questions, receiving silent answers. And they must have been the right answers because his arm tightened around her shoulders and the pressure of his mouth grew more intense.

She responded eagerly to the kiss she'd been waiting

for ever since the first time on the stairs, when he'd backed off so soon. This time he wasn't backing off, but holding her close, caressing her lips with fierce intent, telling her that he wanted her, desired her.

And here, where the darkness gave privacy while heightening every movement and sensation, she could tell him of her own desire, and of the love and longing for him that filled every moment. She could caress his lips with her own, letting him know the things she didn't dare to say. Now there was just the two of them in a place where all feeling was heightened, and everything was possible.

In the din that surrounded them he could hear no more than she, so she was free to whisper his name against his lips. She could gasp as his tongue explored her, surrendering to the exquisite sensation of fire, knowing that he couldn't be sure of anything except what her answering kiss hinted at.

She was gloriously free to do as she liked in the enclosed world of wicked lights and ghastly visions, while joy pervaded her, and skeletons shrieked and gibbered around them.

At last she felt his arm about her shoulders relax, and realised distractedly that they were coming to the end of the ride. They mustn't be seen like this. She separated from him and composed herself just in time. The next moment they'd burst through the curtains into daylight.

And there was Carson, laughing and relaxed, as though nothing had happened.

Had anything happened? Or had it all been nothing but her own fevered imagining? Her lips still burned and her heart was beating fast from the passion that had surged up in her. Yet it seemed to her that Carson showed no sign of disturbance, unless perhaps his hands trembled a little as he helped her out of the car.

Again, Joey demanded eagerly.

'In a minute,' Carson told him. 'I need a moment to recover.' He gave a sudden grin.

'What is it?' Gina asked.

'I was just thinking what I might have been doing this afternoon. Going through the balance sheet, perhaps. On the whole, I think I prefer hooking plastic ducks out of the water.'

As he spoke he was paying the stall keeper for a rod and taking his pick of the ducks that came floating by. He was rewarded by a toy that might have been shaped like a fish, but it was hard to tell.

'What is it?' Carson demanded, studying his prize from various angles.

'Why don't we ask Joey?' Gina looked around and knew a flash of alarm. 'Joey! Carson, he's gone. Oh, my God!'

'Relax,' Carson told her. 'There he is.'

She followed his pointing finger and felt faint with relief as she saw Joey getting into one of the Ghost Train cars. As they moved off he waved at them cheekily. Then the black curtains engulfed him.

'Wretched brat,' Carson said without heat.

'I suppose he simply got tired of waiting for us and decided to strike out on his own,' Gina said. 'I'm glad he feels so confident; it's just—'

'I know,' Carson said with feeling. 'I nearly had a heart attack. Let's fortify ourselves with a cup of tea. There's a little café just over here, and we can keep the Ghost Train in sight.'

Gina sat down at a table while Carson fetched their tea. She felt as though she'd been through a wringer.

There was a queue and it was several minutes before Carson returned. Gina kept her eyes fixed on the Ghost Train and, after a few moments, Joey reappeared. She managed to attract his attention, and he smiled and waved, but didn't get out. He simply gave the man his money, and squeezed over so that a little girl in a red dress could get in beside him.

The man held out his hand to the little girl. She didn't move and the man began to talk, obviously explaining that she couldn't ride if she didn't pay. Joey tapped him on the arm and offered him more money. The man took it, and the cars moved off.

'What are you staring at?' Carson asked, returning with tea.

'I think I've just seen Joey being gallant to a lady.'

She described the incident and Carson grinned. 'He's starting young—just like his old man.'

'You started at eight?'

'I didn't wait that long. When I was seven I was sharing my ice cream with Tilly next door. I can't recall her last name, and even her face is a bit vague. But her appetite for raspberry ripple will stay with me for ever.'

It was good to see him relaxing enough to be humorous. He was casually dressed in a short-sleeved shirt, and the sun had caught him, tanning his face, neck and forearms. For once the tension was gone from his face, and he looked simply a handsome, vital male animal.

There was a small disturbance behind them and they turned to see a man and a woman, both middle-aged, with pleasant, worried faces.

'What are we going to do?' the woman asked frantically.

'Don't fret, Helen. She's probably all right.'

'How can she be all right, so alone and helpless?

Excuse me—' the woman pounced on Gina '—you haven't seen a little girl, have you? She's eight and she's wearing a red dress—she wandered off—'

'Don't worry, I've seen her,' Gina reassured them. 'She went on the Ghost Train. She'll appear in a minute.'

'But she hasn't got any money,' the man said.

'Joey took care of that.'

The couple sat down and introduced themselves as Helen and Peter Leyton.

'Sally's very vulnerable,' Helen explained. 'She's Down's Syndrome.'

At that moment the cars appeared again and drew to a halt. Joey and the little girl were there, sharing the smiles of children who had enjoyed a fantastic adventure. Helen stood up and waved, but she couldn't attract Sally's attention.

'Wait,' Gina said as Helen started forward. 'Let's see what happens. Don't worry about her. She won't come to any harm with Joey.'

'Gina—' Carson protested.

'It's all right. Can't you see he knows what he's doing?'

Joey was handing over more money, evidently having the whole situation under control. As the adults watched he took Sally's hand protectively between both of his, and they were off again.

'Well, I'll be—!' Peter was scratching his head and grinning. 'What a nice kid your son is, Mrs—?'

'He's Mr Page's son. I just look after him,' Gina explained.

'Well, someone's doing a great job,' Helen said. 'He's a real little knight in shining armour. You must be very proud of him.' This was to Carson.

'Yes,' he said quietly. 'I am.'

'It's so good to see Sally making friends with a normal child,' Peter said. 'Most of them flinch away from
her, but your son treats her naturally, and that's what
she needs.' He noticed a strange look on Carson's face.
'Is something wrong?'

'Nothing,' Carson said quickly.

But Gina knew the pleasant shock he'd had at hearing
his son described as a normal child. Because that was
what anyone would think from Joey's bearing. He
wasn't a victim. He was potentially a young man with
a lot of confidence.

'Sally's a darling,' Helen said, 'but she's got a will
of iron. If she wants to do something she tends to wander
off, so we have to look out all the time. This time we
slipped up, I'm afraid.'

'And she has a problem talking,' Peter added. 'Things
don't come out quite right and people don't understand
her. Then she gets upset.'

'We haven't had her long,' Helen put in. 'We're foster
parents, and we specialise in children with problems. It's
a kind of thank-you because our own three are all dis-
gustingly healthy.'

When the cars reappeared they could see that some
sort of dispute was going on. Sally didn't want to get
out. Joey took her arm and urged her, but she wouldn't
budge. At last he climbed over her feet, grasped her hand
firmly and pointed to the café. Faced with this display
of authority, she gave in and meekly followed him, her
hand tucked in his.

Gina looked at Carson's thunderstruck face, and her
lips twitched. 'I'll bet Tilly Whatsername didn't let you
order her about like that,' she said.

'She didn't. The one time I tried, I got ice cream all
over my face.'

Joey appeared at the table with his new friend, and protectively pulled out a chair for her. Sally had a sweet face and myopic eyes behind thick glasses. Her smile was enchanting.

'We're so grateful to you for taking care of her,' Helen said to Joey.

She was looking straight at him, so that he could lip-read easily.

'Could you understand what she said?' Helen added. 'Most people can't, I'm afraid.'

Joey understood this perfectly. His smile contained a hint of mischief, and his eyes went from Gina to Carson, inviting them to share the joke.

'What is it?' Helen asked, catching the look. 'What have I said?'

'Joey's deaf,' Gina explained. 'So Sally's problem doesn't matter to him.'

'Well, I'll be—!' Peter fell back in his chair, scratching his head again. 'I thought I knew about deaf children. We've fostered several. But I never guessed.'

Carson had a strange look on his face. 'My son has great style,' he said simply.

'Yes,' Gina said eagerly. 'That's the word. Style.'

Peter began to sign, introducing himself, Helen and Sally. Joey nodded and returned the courtesy, but he was interrupted by Sally, who pulled his shirt to indicate that she wanted something.

Can we have some ice cream? he signed. *Strawberry for Sally and chocolate for me.*

'How do you know Sally wants strawberry?' Gina asked.

I'll give it to her. She'll like it.

And she would, Gina realised. She would like whatever Joey gave her, because it came from him. The little boy had found exactly what he needed—someone with bigger problems than his own. And, before their eyes, he was growing to meet the challenge.

She met Carson's gaze and found there what she'd hoped for—pure fatherly pride. His grin had a touch of self-consciousness, but the pride was unmistakable.

Before they parted, that evening, they made plans to meet up with the Leytons next day. Joey's eyelids were drooping, and after a meal he was ready for bed. Gina left father and son to say their goodnights, while she wandered down to the lobby and browsed the book stall. She bought a showbiz 'news' magazine, and looked idly through the pages, until she found a headline that made her stiffen.

Angelica Duvaine—on the slippery slope?

The story that followed was written in tones of sympathy that dripped with malice. After her role in the blockbuster Angelica's career hadn't taken off as expected. Good parts were thin on the ground. A TV project had just fallen through. Her romance with a notable producer had ended suddenly.

Gina let the magazine fall into the waste bin. Suddenly she felt uneasy.

CHAPTER TEN

AFTER that the two parties met up at least once a day. Every morning began with a visit to the aquarium. Joey was a favourite with the staff, who became used to talking to suit him. Carson and Gina had little to do but linger in the background in case they were needed.

One morning, when Joey was engaged in an earnest discussion, Carson said, 'Do you feel safe leaving him in the care of the Leytons?'

'Of course. They look after him as well as we can. Why?'

'They're taking Sally back to the funfair tonight, and for a pizza afterwards, and they'd like him to go too. I thought you and I could have a meal together.'

'That would be lovely.'

'Great. Now, if Einstein over there has finished, I need a cup of tea.'

That evening, as he was dressing in smart clothes for the restaurant, Carson saw Joey in the mirror, standing in his doorway, and beckoned him over.

'Are you looking forward to tonight?' he asked.

Joey nodded.

We're going to the funfair and I'm going to take Sally on the Ghost Train.

'Good. Here.' He put some money into Joey's hand. 'Buy her some ice cream as well. Girls like it.' He winked at his son. 'I know.'

As Joey turned to go something seemed to hold him back. He looked at the carpet, then at his father. His whole body radiated awkwardness mingled with determination.

'What is it?' Carson asked.

Do you like Gina?

Carson nodded. 'Of course.'

Joey spread his fingers and moved his hands back and forth to each other. *A lot?*

'Yes, a lot.'

Keeping his fingers wide, Joey changed the angle of his hands so that they were flat, and moved them up and down, keeping his eyes on his father.

'Yes,' Carson said, understanding. 'Lots and lots.'

The movements became more vigorous, and his eyebrows were raised in enquiry. *More than lots?*

'That's enough,' Carson said hastily. 'I like her; let's leave it there.' He met his son's eye. 'How about you?'

Lots and lots and lots.

To Carson's great relief, there was a knock on the door and Gina appeared, followed by the Leytons.

'Better give us the number of your mobile,' Helen said, 'just in case of emergencies. Right, folks! Let's be off.'

Carson had half expected Gina to appear in the chiffon she'd worn the night of Dan's ill-fated proposal. Instead she'd chosen something soft and dark blue that he hadn't seen before. And now he realised that he wouldn't have liked her in a dress she'd worn for another man.

It was a warm evening and they strolled along the seafront, pausing to lean on the rail and watch the tiny waves breaking on the sand as the tide went out.

'What were you and Joey talking about when I came in?' Gina asked.

He was about to answer when it dawned on him that he could hardly repeat that particular conversation.

'This and that,' he said vaguely. 'I forget the details.
Let's go and have that meal.'

To her relief he'd found a quiet restaurant, with very
little background noise.

'Is this all right for you?' he asked anxiously.

'This is fine,' she said happily. 'It really helps when
someone thinks of these things.'

'How ever did you manage in Bob's Café that first
day? There was a hell of a din in the background.'

'I'm used to the din there. I can sort of screen it out
now. And I filled in the gaps with a bit of lip-reading.'

'I can't get my head round the way you're so cool
about it.'

'The trick is not to let it be a bigger problem than it
needs to be,' she said seriously. Then she chuckled suddenly. 'And it can be useful sometimes.'

'I don't believe that.'

'No, really. I went on holiday to Spain with some
friends, and the next-door hotel wasn't finished yet. They
were drilling and pounding all night, and everyone was
going crazy because they were being kept awake. Me, I
just switched everything off and went to sleep.'

He laughed, regarding her with admiration. 'You're
unbelievable.'

While he was talking to the waiter Gina leaned back
in her chair, revelling in the unexpected pleasure of this
evening. Through the window by their table she could
see the ocean, blue and tranquil in the twilight. Coloured
lamps were coming on all down the promenade, giving
the scene an air of ghostly charm.

Sitting opposite her was the man she loved. And he
was all hers for the evening.

'When is Joey's device due to be switched on?' he
asked.

'In ten days.'

'Three days before his eighth birthday,' Carson mused. 'We'll really have something to celebrate!'

'But don't let Joey think you're expecting miracles, or that you're disappointed when they don't happen. He'll hear things but it'll be very disorganised at first.'

'I know. But it'll be a great birthday. There'll be hope again.'

'I wonder if Joey understands about hope? He's never really had any.'

'Except the false hopes he clings to about Brenda,' Carson sighed. 'Our divorce becomes final a week after his birthday. Almost nine years to the day since we married.'

'Do you mind?' she ventured to ask.

'The past is the past. Let it go.'

She watched him with jealous eyes, wondering if there wasn't a shadow of regret in his tone. Could he let it go as easily as he said?

'I've been meaning to ask you,' he said. 'What did Joey say just before we left home the other day? I asked him what we should call you, and he made a sign I couldn't follow.'

'It was the sign for "mother",' Gina said.

'That's how he sees you?'

'In a sort of way.'

Carson took his eyes off her for a moment, as though debating with himself, then looked back with an air of resolution.

'Maybe Joey knows what he's talking about.'

'Well, I've fallen into the role Brenda ought to occupy—'

'That's not what I meant. You told me to put his needs first, and what he needs is you—as his mother.'

'But I'm not his mother.'

'You could be—if we got married.' He heard her gasp and hurried on, 'It's not impossible, is it? We make a perfect family, you—and me—and Joey.'

'Carson—' Her head was whirling.

'If I believed in fate I'd say it was fate that we met. Joey saw it at once; he turned to you the first moment. He needs you, and I—'

'Yes?'

'You know that I need you. Who do I turn to when things get tough? The same person as Joey. I don't think I could manage without you now.' He made a sound of impatience. 'Hell! Listen to me, sounding like another child clinging to your skirts.'

'No, I'd never think that of you,' she said with a faint smile. 'And there are worse things in the world than being needed.'

'Yes, but there's more than that. I'd be a good husband, Gina, I swear it. I'd do my best to make you happy. You've come to mean a great deal to me. I wonder if you know that?'

'Well, I do have certain memories of the Ghost Train.'

His smile almost stopped her heart. 'You never said anything. I wondered if you'd even noticed.'

'Oh, yes, I noticed...'

She was playing for time, waiting for him to say the words she longed for. 'You've come to mean a great deal to me' wasn't enough. She loved him so much that the sight of him sitting there, so handsome and vital, watching her with a warm look in his eyes, almost made her throw caution to the winds and accept him now. But a wise instinct stopped her.

'But when you didn't say anything,' she went on, 'I thought I'd imagined it.'

'You didn't, and I don't think I imagined that you kissed me back. We could make a very good marriage. A lot of couples don't have nearly as much going for them as we do.'

Except that they love each other, she thought wistfully.

He took her hand in his, caressing the back lightly with his thumb. 'You really did kiss me back. I felt it. I believe I could please you. Don't you think we could be happy?'

It could be so blissful that I could die of happiness, she thought. But not for long. Not when the difference between my love and your mild affection began to gape.

When she didn't answer he let her hand fall.

'I'm sorry,' he said. 'I guess I got it all wrong.'

She longed to ask him if he only wanted her for Joey's sake, and because they had so much going for them. But what would be the point of asking, when he'd already as good as told her?

'You didn't get it wrong,' she said at last. 'But I can't answer now. Give me until tomorrow.'

'Of course. You're right. It's a big decision, but to me it seems so inevitable that I hoped you might have thought of it too.'

Since he'd held her in his arms she'd thought constantly of marrying him. She'd hoped and dreamed, and now the dream was coming true. And it was all wrong.

They walked back slowly along the edge of the beach, where the sand was firm. Carson held her hand quietly in his. He didn't speak of marriage again and she thought he meant to let the subject go for a while, but when they came to where they would have to leave the beach he suddenly pulled her into the shadows, and into his arms.

'Gina...' he said against her lips, and she heard him

less with her ears than with her heart. 'Kiss me—let me feel you kiss me—'

'Carson, please—'

'This is right for us,' he growled. 'I know it is. Trust me.'

There was purpose in his lips, almost as though he were arguing with her, telling her how good things could be between them. He was telling her, too, that he was in control, and wasn't going to let her refuse him what he wanted. It was hard for her to protest when her heart and senses betrayed her to him with every flicker of his tongue.

She should stand up to him, refuse to let him dominate her as he was trying to do. But she wanted to be nowhere but here, doing nothing else but kissing him to distraction. Denying him was denying herself.

She found herself responding passionately, in defiance of her own warnings. She would be sensible soon, but not yet. First she would give herself this lovely moment, perhaps the last she would ever have.

He knew how to make it hard for her, kissing her with such ardour and tenderness that she nearly yielded there and then. 'Say yes,' he whispered. 'Be sensible and say yes, Gina.'

'Sensible!' she gasped.

'It's what we both want. It can work so well.' He relaxed his hold, so that he could see her face clearly. Her breasts were rising and falling with the desire he'd inflamed so easily, so efficiently—for Carson Page was always efficient about getting his own way. Perhaps he guessed how close she was to yielding, but he mustn't be allowed to know any more.

'If I had my way,' he said, 'I'd take you to bed now

and make love to you until you were convinced. Won't you let me do that?'

She fought down the longing to throw herself back into his arms and say, Yes, yes! and shook her head stubbornly. 'You're talking about the rest of our lives,' she said. 'Not—not—this is just a moment. I won't decide this way. Let me go, Carson, please.'

With a puzzled frown, he did so. She took a few steps away from him and leaned against a breakwater, keeping her face hidden lest he discover how distraught she was.

Why couldn't she just give in? she thought despairingly. Why was she cursed with a mind that asked awkward questions when she only wanted to surrender to her heart?

'I'm sorry, Gina,' Carson said at last. 'I didn't mean to upset—or offend—you.'

She pulled herself together and managed a watery laugh. 'It's all right. I'm not offended, but you did rather try to steamroller over me.'

'I'm afraid I'm like that. It gets results in business, but I guess it's no way to woo a lady.'

You're not wooing me, she thought sadly. You're making a take-over bid for a useful asset. If only...

'Have I blown my chances?' he asked. 'Does this mean the answer's no?'

'I didn't say that—but you said I could have until tomorrow. A deal's a deal.'

'Yes. I'm sorry. Let's walk back to the hotel. Give me your hand. I promise you're quite safe.'

He tucked her hand into the crook of his arm and they walked sedately back to the hotel. He looked into her room for a moment to check on Joey. When he saw the child was soundly asleep he gave her a brief smile, and was gone.

* * *

The hours of the night passed slowly, until the first light appeared, and she got up to sit by the window. The man she loved had asked her to marry him, and it should have been her happiest moment. But her heart was heavy.

If only she could silence the memory of Carson saying, 'Infatuation is a bad basis for marriage. The best one is if people have something in common and are fond of each other—but, even then, not too fond.'

There it was, what he was offering her—marriage at a cautious distance. A sensible arrangement between two people who wouldn't ask much of each other. Shared interests, some physical pleasure, but no love because he had none to give, except to a little boy. And how long would pleasure survive when she'd looked too often into its hollow heart?

But then, to leave him… Never to see him again because she'd been too proud to take the little that was offered and make the best of it.

Why give up so soon? Surely she could win his love, in time?

His love, perhaps, but not the all-absorbing passion he'd given to Brenda. Could she marry him and avoid destroying them both with the demon of jealousy?

Back and forth her thoughts went until she felt as though they would tear her in two. At last she leaned her head against the cold window, dozing unhappily in the dawn light. Joey found her like that when he awoke.

There was something unnatural about the day that followed. Gina and Carson went through a parade of acting normally, as though their minds weren't both dominated by the same thought.

The Leytons were leaving that afternoon, and a final meeting for coffee and a visit to the fair got them through some of the day. After putting Joey to bed, Gina and Carson were to eat downstairs in the restaurant.

'Will you be all right?' she asked the child. 'We'll only be downstairs, but if you wake and we're not here—'

I'll go back to sleep again, was his common-sense answer.

'Yes, I'm fussing too much,' she said, reading the subtext beneath the signing. Joey grinned his agreement, and a moment later he was asleep.

Over dinner they talked about this and that, continuing the pretence of the day until their invention ran out. She looked up to find Carson watching her.

'Don't you have an answer for me?' he asked.

'You must think I'm a dithering idiot,' she said with a sigh. 'I've been thinking and thinking—'

'Is it such a terrible prospect that you have to talk yourself into it?'

'No, but—just a little more time, Carson, please.'

'Of course,' he said courteously. 'If you've finished, we might take a stroll.'

The waiter brought the bill and he signed for it. Then he patted his pocket, annoyed with himself.

'I've left my wallet behind. I'd better get it before we go out.'

He hurried upstairs, collected the wallet from his room and headed back, but as he passed Joey's room something stopped him. From inside he could hear a soft noise, almost like whimpering. Frowning, he pushed open the door. The light was off and Joey was hunched under the bedclothes, moving about jerkily and making the sounds Carson had heard outside. There was something desperate about them.

He moved to the bed and touched his son on the

shoulder, shaking him gently. But Joey seemed in the grip of a nightmare. He moaned more loudly, but his eyes stayed closed. Carson shook him again, and this time the boy shuddered and his eyes opened.

But instead of focusing on his father they stared wildly into the distance. His chest heaved and tears poured down his face.

Sorrow wrenched at Carson's heart. This was his child, in distress, and he couldn't help him. He put the bedside light on so that Joey could see him, and grasped the boy firmly to get his attention. At last, to his relief, the child's eyes seemed to find him.

'Joey,' he said, slowly and clearly. 'It's all right. It's over now. Joey—it's over.'

What had scared the child so badly in his sleep that he couldn't shake it off now? If only Gina were here. She would know what to do.

But she wasn't. There was only himself to comfort his son, and he was failing him, as always. In pain and helplessness he drew the little boy against him and enfolded him in his arms.

'There, there,' he said. 'There, there.'

He felt the soft brush of fingers against his neck. Joey had reached up until his hand could fit against his father's throat. He pressed gently, not enough to hurt, but enough to feel the vibration.

'I'm here,' Carson said again. 'It's all right. Daddy's here—Daddy's here.'

He didn't know if Joey could make out the words, or whether it meant anything to him at all, but he kept on making sounds of comfort, and gradually he felt his child relax. He looked down.

Joey had fallen asleep trustingly in his arms.

For a long time he watched the little boy's face, a

prey to feelings that shook him fiercely and left him drained. The pent-up love of years was there, waiting to break down the barriers of fear and incomprehension.

There was a soft noise in the doorway, and Gina slipped inside. When she saw father and son she stayed very still, watching them, smiling. Carson looked up.

'He was having a nightmare. I don't think I can go out after all. If he awakens—'

'He must find you still here,' she agreed at once, coming over to the bed.

Joey stirred again and Carson looked down into the child's face. Gina drew a long, wondering breath at the expression on his face. This was the real Carson, the man who lived beneath the prickly exterior, a man whose love for his son was so profound and heartbreaking that it could barely be confessed, and then only to herself.

She'd come close to refusing him but now she saw that she'd nearly thrown away everything that made her life worth living. Their marriage might bring her sadness, but she loved this vulnerable man, and she could no more walk away from him than fly to the moon. Whatever the future held, she would face it.

She touched him gently on the shoulder and waited for him to look up.

'I'll marry you,' she said.

She slept in Carson's room that night, so that he could be with his son. Next morning, she knocked on their door early. She had something important to say.

'Is Joey awake?'

'Yes.'

'Did he tell you what was the matter last night?'

'He doesn't even remember having a nightmare.'

'Then you must have driven it right away. Carson, have you told him about us?'

'No, I wanted you to be there to see his face.'

'I don't want to tell him just yet. Let's wait until he's been switched on. He's got a lot on his plate.'

'Maybe you're right,' Carson agreed reluctantly.

It was the last morning, and in the afternoon they would start the journey home. Their final visit to the funfair was marred by one painful incident. But Gina thought that if you looked at it the right way it was a kind of triumph.

Joey became absorbed in hooking ducks out of the water. There was another boy there, of about his own age, and it soon developed into a contest between them. The boy's parents looked on, smiling.

But their smiles changed to frowns when the children began to talk. Joey ventured to try speaking a few words, which the other boy seemed to comprehend. But his parents looked uncomfortable, and the mother moved forward and took firm hold of her son's arm.

'Come along, darling. We've got to be getting on.'

'Mum—' the child tried to introduce his new friend '—this is Joey—'

'Yes, dear, but we have to be going.'

'But Mum—'

'Come on!' the mother snapped. 'Leave him alone, dear. He isn't like other children.'

She spoke slowly and emphatically, and Joey, watching her face, made out every word. Gina flinched at the look that washed over his face.

But she wasn't the only one who'd seen it. Carson confronted the woman, barely containing his rage.

'You're right, madam,' he said bitingly. 'My son isn't

like other children. He has more brains, more courage and more sheer guts than most people will ever know.'

It was worth everything to see the change in Joey as he saw his father defending him. He understood everything, not just the words, but Carson's attitude of fierce protectiveness, and the way he laid his hand on his shoulder.

The other couple gathered their son and scuttled away. Joey and Carson looked at each other.

'Are you all right, son?'

Joey nodded, and slipped his hand confidingly into his father's. There was a shining happiness about him, and it lasted all the way home.

CHAPTER ELEVEN

ON THE day of Joey's 'switch-on' Carson drove them to the hospital. Joey sat in the back of the car with Gina, attending while she silently explained that today he would see, not a doctor, but a hearing specialist called an aurologist and a speech therapist. By the time they entered the building he had the air of someone who understood that serious business was afoot.

Gina had feared that the exterior attachment and the process of switching on and testing the sound might be distressing to a child. But Joey was so eager to get on that he took it all in his stride. At last the aurologist had finished.

'Now,' he said, standing back, 'let's see what happens.'

Nothing.

Joey looked around him in bewilderment, as if asking what was supposed to happen next. Gina closed her eyes, praying hard. Carson's face was deathly pale. He turned away and went to the window behind his son. When he looked back Joey was sitting with his head bent, as though crushed by defeat.

'My God!' he said, distraught. 'Oh, my God!'

Joey swung around sharply to look at his father.

'Carson,' Gina said through tears of joy. 'He heard you!'

'Did you?' Carson flung himself on his knees beside Joey. 'Did you hear me?'

'He can't understand,' Gina protested. 'He's not used to the sounds of the words.'

Carson took Joey's face between his hands, looking at him steadily. 'Joey,' he said. 'Joey.'

'Aaaah—' the child said. And suddenly, a light came into his face. He had heard his own voice.

'Joey,' Carson repeated, hardly daring to believe the miracle

'Aaaah!' Joey repeated the sound, his astonishment and delight wonderful to see. 'Aaaahh!' he yelled jubilantly, while everyone in the room smiled and covered their ears.

'He did it,' Carson said in triumph. 'He can hear!'

The aurologist was smiling but cautious. 'Now the real work begins,' he said. 'The mapping is going to take time.'

'Mapping?' Carson echoed.

'Programming the device so that Joey gets the best results. The levels and the tuning vary from person to person. You'll need to bring him back every week, then every two weeks, then every month, every two months, three months, six, then once a year. And each time we'll adjust the sound, building on his experience.'

He and Joey set to work, testing noises, constantly adjusting until they found the level where Joey was comfortable.

After a while Gina looked around and realised that Carson was missing. She slipped out into the corridor and found him there, standing, leaning against the wall, his eyes closed. He looked almost more like a man crushed by misfortune than one who'd seen the dawn of hope, but she knew him now, and understood the violence of the emotion that racked him.

She went to his side and touched him. At once his

arms went tightly about her, and they stood together in
the quiet corridor while his shoulders heaved with sobs.

Gina made Joey's birthday cake herself and lovingly
adorned it with eight candles.

She put the finishing touches to it early in the morning
before Joey was up. Carson too came down early and
found her in the kitchen. She was carefully adjusting the
last candle, and he slipped his arms around her from
behind, kissing the back of her neck in a way that distracted her and sent the candle toppling to the floor.

'Now look what you've done,' she told him severely.

'You've got plenty more candles. You can spare me
a moment, can't you?'

She emerged from his arms a few minutes later,
breathless and somewhat dishevelled.

'No more waiting,' he said. 'I want to tell Joey about
us today. We can be married by the end of next month.
Say yes.'

'Yes,' she said happily. To be his wife in a few weeks.
What more could she ask?

The sound of footsteps alerted them. Gina hastily
whisked the cake out of sight, and a moment later Joey
burst in gleefully. After that it was a pandemonium of
laughter and presents.

The three of them spent the day in the park. It was
the merriest birthday Joey had ever known. The world
was a wonderland of new sounds. Some of them confused him, and he couldn't cope with too many at once.
But he was learning all the time.

In the late afternoon they returned home and Gina set
up the table for tea. The cake was a triumphant success
as she carried it in with the candles alight.

'Blow!' she said.

Joey took a huge breath and blew all eight candles out at once, while the other two clapped. When they had all eaten a slice Carson gave her a questioning look, which she answered with a nod. The child looked from one to the other.

'Joey,' Carson said, 'you know how important Gina has become to us?' Joey nodded. 'Well, what would you say if——?'

He was interrupted by a sharp rap on the window behind them. Outside was a beautiful young woman with blonde hair, knocking with one hand and waving with the other. Through the net curtains Gina couldn't see her clearly at first.

But then she did. And, with horror, she recognised her.

Angelica Duvaine.

Suddenly everything seemed to be in slow motion: Carson, following her appalled gaze, growing tense and still; Joey, his eyes riveted on the window, his mouth silently forming the word 'Mummy'.

Carson rose like a man in a dream. He seemed to find it hard to move. Gina was watching his face, but all it contained was disbelief.

Joey was the first to come to life. He jumped to his feet and raced to the door, pulling it open to throw himself into the wide open arms of the woman. Carson seemed to recover the power of movement and went after him. Gina followed and was just in time to see Angelica put her arms about him, kissing him lingeringly on the mouth, while Joey bounced with excitement, and a dozen photographers snapped away eagerly.

Angelica Duvaine had brought the press with her.

'Damn you, get out of here!' Carson roared at them.

'Don't be angry, darling,' Angelica cooed in a seductive voice. 'I just had to share our happiness with the world.'

She turned from him quickly and hugged Joey again, the picture of motherly delight, but with her face always carefully turned towards the cameras.

A man wielding a microphone pushed forward. 'Do you have a statement for us, Miss Duvaine?'

'Only that this is the happiest day of my life. All my sadness is over—'

'Get in the house,' Carson said in a savage undervoice.

'I have to be going now,' she told the journalist. 'I need to be alone with my family—I'm sure you understand—'

She managed to tuck one hand in Carson's arm and use the other to draw Joey against her, and the three of them went into the house. Gina backed away to let them in, and she could feel the other woman's eyes flickering coldly over her, not missing a thing.

But she didn't waste words on Gina. As soon as the door was closed she forestalled Carson's explosion by dropping to her knees and embracing Joey with cooing sounds of delight. The child clung to his mother in a way that said everything about his loneliness and sense of abandonment.

Gina watched, realising that she had been fooling herself. She'd got as close to Joey as she could, and he'd become fond of her, but it was all as nothing the moment his real mother returned.

And Carson? Would it be the same with him? Would he forget her now that the woman he'd once loved so terribly had come back?

She was dizzy was the suddenness with which the world had turned around. One moment Carson had been announcing their engagement; the next, Angelica was there in their midst, reclaiming him and their son with terrifying confidence.

'Oh, it's so good to be home!' she cried dramatically.

'You still have a key, I seem to recall,' Carson said in a biting voice. 'You could simply have walked in.'

'Oh, that wouldn't have been nearly so effective, darling.'

'No, it wouldn't have got us all out there where the press could see us, would it?' he snapped.

'Well, you must admit, they were lovely shots.'

'How dare you do such a thing to Joey?'

'Joey didn't mind, did you, darling?'

The child was trying to cope with a host of unfamiliar noises. He made a sound that Gina understood but which caused his mother to look down at him with a frown.

'What?' she asked, a tad sharply.

'He said "Mummy",' Gina told her quietly.

Angelica straightened, and looked Gina up and down with deep, deep blue eyes. Her beautiful mouth twitched as though she'd seen something funny. And Gina, who until then had thought herself smartly dressed, knew that she was a little brown mouse after all.

'I don't believe we've been introduced,' Angelica cooed.

'My name is Gina Tennison,' she said, pulling herself together. 'I'm here because I can help Joey.'

Before Gina could stop her the film star enveloped her in a scented embrace.

'Then you're my friend,' she said in accents of passionate sincerity. 'Anyone who helps my dear little son is my friend, as I am hers.'

'You ought to know, Brenda,' Carson broke in harshly, 'that Gina is a great deal more than—'

'Carson.' Gina stopped him in a voice that was half a plea, half a warning. 'Not now.'

Angelica's narrowed eyes flickered between them. She wasn't an intelligent woman, but she had a stiletto-sharp instinct where her own interests were concerned. Carson's words had been revealing, but the way Gina felt free to interrupt him, and the familiarity of that, 'Not now,' alerted her far more.

She kept her smile in place to say, 'Tell me about yourself. You're some kind of speech therapist?'

'No, I'm a lawyer. But I'm deaf.'

'Oh, really? You must be wonderful at lip-reading. I thought you could hear.'

'I can hear, because I have a cochlear implant, just like Joey. But I'm still deaf, just as he is.'

Angelica gave a trill of disbelieving laughter. 'Non-sense. Joey isn't deaf any more. He's been cured.'

'There is no cure,' Gina said firmly. 'Joey is as deaf as he ever was. With time and a lot of work he'll pass as what you call "normal".' For the life of her, she couldn't have kept a tinge of contempt out of the last four words. 'But he'll still be deaf.'

'Really?' Angelica said frostily. 'That's not quite what I—well, never mind. I'm sure we'll all manage some-how.'

'We?' Carson asked ominously.

'Well, we are a family, darling,' Angelica said sweetly. 'You, me and our little son. And family reunions are happy occasions.'

Carson's face was pale. 'What the devil brought you back here, Brenda?'

She winced. 'I do wish you wouldn't use that name. It's not me.'

'I said, what brought you back here? Why this sudden display of maternal concern?'

Angelica shrugged, beautifully. 'Well, my dear, it's expected, especially if— Oh, hell! Some stupid cow from *Movie Enquirer* picked up a hint and thought she'd make trouble for me.'

'They've found out, haven't they?' Carson said savagely. 'Someone in that self-centred little hell-hole you live in has heard about Joey and is asking awkward questions—like how could the beautiful Angelica Duvaine desert a sick child? And suddenly you don't look so good.'

Angelica shrugged again. 'Put it how you like. I'm here now and there's nothing you can do about it.'

'Can't I? I could have you out of that door so fast—'

'Oh, I don't think Joey would like that,' she replied, turning her wide eyes on him. 'Would you?'

Carson was speechless. It was Gina who answered.

'No,' she said. 'Joey wouldn't like that at all.'

Carson wheeled on her. 'Can't you see the game she's playing?'

'Of course I can see it. But you have to go along with it, at least for the moment.'

'He'll go along with it for as long as it suits me,' Angelica snapped at her. 'Now, if you wouldn't mind leaving us, I need to have a long, private talk with *my husband*.'

'I'm no husband of yours,' Carson said. 'Our marriage was over long ago.'

'Not according to the law. There are papers that make it very clear that we are still husband and wife for the next few days, at least.'

'After which our divorce will become final,' Carson said firmly.

'Why don't we talk about that later? I just want to enjoy my little boy's birthday.'

She had come with a mountain of presents, which she unloaded onto the child, apparently oblivious of the fact that her presence was enough to make him happy. Joey exclaimed over the parcels and tried, haltingly, to thank her. The few words he could manage came out distorted, and Gina had to interpret for him, while Brenda's smile grew more frayed.

But she persevered, covering Joey with kisses at regular intervals. The child looked up, beaming first at his mother, then at his father. To him, this was the longed-for family reunion.

Gina turned away from that sight. Her heart was heavy.

The house was very quiet and dark. Gina had undressed for bed, but although she lay down for a while she didn't expect to sleep, and soon rose again.

A glance into Joey's room showed her that he was asleep. Brenda had made a great performance of putting him to bed, and if there was anything missing in her attitude he didn't seem to notice.

Perhaps, Gina thought, the actress still had some genuine, motherly feeling for him. For Joey's sake, she would have been glad to believe it.

Gina had slipped away to her room without trying to talk to Carson. Now she wondered where he was. In his bedroom, presumably. And Angelica? Where was she?

She'd forgotten to bring a glass of water upstairs as she normally did. Pulling on her dressing gown, she slipped out into the corridor and headed down the stairs to the kitchen.

There was a faint light in the hall downstairs, coming

from beyond an open door. As Gina reached the bottom step she froze, realising that she'd been mistaken. Angelica and Carson weren't in his bedroom at all. Through the door to the front room she could see them, in each other's arms.

At first everything was a confused jumble—two bodies pressed together—two mouths locked—Angelica half naked in a seductive diaphanous creation—hands embracing, caressing, inciting to passion—

Then Gina's head cleared and she saw that Carson's arms were by his sides. It was Angelica's hands that writhed, sliding over his head, his shoulders, vainly trying to rekindle desire. The man stood motionless, coldly waiting for her to be finished.

Eventually Angelica drew back, her lovely mouth curved in laughing disbelief.

'Don't be so stuffy, darling. You and I always had the hots for each other, and some things simply don't die. I've thought of you a lot recently—'

Carson didn't move and he didn't speak.

'Oh, sweetie, are you trying to punish me? Playing hard to get? Well, that might even be rather fun. Remember how we used to—?'

'Shut up and get out, Brenda.' Carson's voice was like ice as he pushed her away from him. 'And don't try to touch me again or I'll make you very sorry.'

'You're afraid,' she jeered. 'You know you can't resist me.'

'I think I've just proved that I can. No, it's simpler than that. You make my skin crawl. All I can think of is the rottenness inside you.'

'I see. It's Miss Goody Two-Shoes now, is it?'

'I'm going to marry Gina, yes. And we'll have a real marriage, which is more than you and I ever had.'

'Oh, you're so smug and sure of yourself. That was always what I couldn't stand about you. Well, don't make any plans for an early marriage. It doesn't suit me to be divorced just yet. It wouldn't go well with the reconciliation story I've given the press.

'But one day—who knows? Be nice to me, and in the end I'll probably be nice to you. In the meantime, we can always—'

She slipped a silk-clad arm about his neck again and tried to fasten her mouth on his, but Carson moved fast, fending her off with a gesture so vigorous that it sent her reeling back to land sprawling in an undignified heap on the sofa.

'You son of a bitch!' she shrieked. 'In Hollywood they queue up to sleep with me. I've had—' She began to reel off a string of names.

But she was talking to air. Carson had walked out of the room.

Gina saw him coming and backed up the stairs. He found her at the top, leaning against the wall, almost dizzy from what she'd witnessed.

'How much of that did you see?' Carson asked her.

'I saw her trying to kiss you—'

'Then you also saw me reject her. I couldn't sleep with her if she was the last woman on earth. She makes me ill. Don't tell me you doubted that?' He looked more closely and saw her eyes shining with tears. 'What a fool you are, my darling!' he said gently. 'Did you really think she could get me back to her bed?'

'I wondered,' she said huskily.

'Well, now you know better.'

A movement from below made him draw her away to his room. When they were inside he locked the door and put his hands on her shoulders, looking into her face by the pale light coming through the window.

'You really believed that of me?' he asked. 'We're to be married soon, and you thought I'd take another woman to my bed?'

'Brenda isn't just another woman. I've heard you talk about her, like an obsession that would haunt you for ever.'

'Maybe she was, once. A sick obsession. But sickness can be healed. I'm a different man now, whole and sane because you came to me with your generosity, your courage and your laughter. I'd forgotten about laughter until I met you with your crazy little car. I'd forgotten about love until I held you in my arms.'

He drew her closer. 'Now, this is all I want. Let that woman do her damnedest! She won't part us.'

'But, Carson, don't you realise that—?'

'Forget her,' he said against her mouth.

With a sinking heart Gina realised that Carson hadn't discerned the bleak truth that faced them. Angelica had already done her damnedest, and it was enough to make their life together impossible.

But the feel of his lips was wonderful, creating heat and passion, so that the sad thoughts faded. There would be a lifetime for them later. Just now she would surrender to her love, and lay up for herself memories to cherish like treasure in the cold, lonely time ahead: the time that she had seen, and he hadn't.

Slowly, almost reverently, he drew off her nightdress, revealing the whole of her slim, pale body.

'Do you know how long—and how badly—I've wanted you?' he murmured.

Gina shook her head. 'I only wish I did.'

'Then let me show you.'

He pulled off his own clothes, kicked them impatiently aside, and drew her nakedness against his own. The first touch was like fire for them both. His kiss was deep and intense, taking possession of her. She leaned against him, glad to yield to her desire, eager to belong to him totally in the flesh as she did in spirit.

She felt his body along the length of her own, pressing her close, and she held him, running her hands over his long, muscular back, down the length of his spine to the lean, powerful hips and thighs. Tremors went through him at the touch of her fingers, gentle at first, then inciting him as she grew in confidence.

His tension grew as he sensed her caresses asking for his love, and he lifted her, carrying her the short distance to his big bed, and laying her down tenderly. He didn't rush her, but contemplated every line and curve of her beauty before dropping his head to lay between her breasts.

She had known nothing like the sensation of his lips loving and teasing her nipples while she took long, ecstatic breaths. She couldn't have said where love ended and desire began. For this man alone, they were one and the same.

She had feared Carson's passion was dead, but now she saw his fierce, growing urgency, and knew that what Angelica Duvaine had striven in vain to rouse was hers for the asking.

When he came over her she was ready, sweet and welcoming, offering him all she had. The feel of him inside her was wonderful. She was right to have claimed this moment, perhaps all she would ever know of love. She held him to her passionately, seeking to imprint every detail of his body on her memory.

The smooth back under her hands would be with her

always, as would the breadth of his shoulders, and the heat of his skin against hers. But what would live with her longest was the memory of being one with him, of being his utterly and completely in a union of body, soul and heart.

She held him closer, whispering his name, nothing held back, no defences. All his. His in every way. When the moment came she tried vainly to hold onto it, and wept as it slipped away. For other lovers there was the promise of next time, but not for her.

Carson kissed her face until her tears had dried, smiling at her in the moonlight.

'Now you belong to me for ever,' he said.

'Yes,' she said huskily. 'I'll always belong to you, wherever I am, wherever you are.'

'What are you talking about? We're not going to be apart. We're going to be married.'

'But we *can't* be married,' she said despairingly. 'My darling, haven't you understood that I have to go away and leave you, and that we may never see each other again?'

CHAPTER TWELVE

CARSON frowned as if he couldn't comprehend her meaning.

'What do you mean?' he asked. 'This is a beginning for us. You can't leave me now.' His voice was arrogant with possessiveness. 'I won't allow it.'

She rested her face against him, willing the world to vanish. If only he could order this as he ordered so many things.

'Don't you realise that it's gone beyond that?' she asked huskily. 'It's out of our hands. Oh, darling, I wish I could see some hope for us, but I can't.'

He stared at her in disbelief. 'You can't mean that,' he said at last. 'Forget what Brenda said about still being married to me—'

'It's not Brenda, it's Joey. He wants his family back, and he thinks he has it. Haven't you seen how happy he is?'

'He's in a fool's paradise. Gina, don't talk like this. Don't make us all suffer because that woman has taken you in.'

'She hasn't taken me in,' she answered in a shaking voice. 'I see exactly what she is. But I also saw Joey's face when she appeared.

'When my mother died, for months afterwards I told myself that she hadn't really gone for good, that one day she'd forgive me for being "a bad girl", and come home. I pictured it again and again, how the door would open, and there she'd be. And I'd run to her, and she'd hold me. She was dead, but that didn't stop me imagining it.

'And today it was there in Joey's eyes, everything I'd been thinking and feeling. His dream came true.'

'But it's only a few days ago that he was talking of you as his mother.'

'Only as a substitute. Now he's got the real thing, and for the first time he's completely happy. I won't be the one to take that happiness away from him.'

'No, Brenda will do that.'

'Then he'll have you to make it up to him. You'll have to stick close by them both, make her behave herself, help him when she doesn't.'

He tore his hair. 'This will all be over in a few days. She'll rush back to Los Angeles——'

'I don't think we can count on that. She's going through a rough patch. She lost that TV show. Darling, however long it takes, let Joey enjoy his happiness while he can. You can help now. You two have found each other.'

'Only because of you.'

'Yes, maybe because of me. I'd like to think so. You'll both be all right now.'

'Will we?' he said bitterly. 'Do you think I can love you as deeply as I do, and be *all right* without you? My God, I knew you didn't love me as I love you, but I expected more than that!'

'You love me?' she whispered. 'And you think—you actually think—that I don't love you?'

'It was all for Joey, wasn't it? And because you want to put right the wrongs of your own childhood. You would have married me for Joey's sake, and now you're leaving me for Joey's sake.'

'But—' she searched his face, hardly able to believe

what she'd just heard '—of course it wasn't just for Joey's sake. How could you believe that?'

'Because you took so long to say you'd marry me. You only agreed when he had that nightmare. I knew what to read into that.'

'Then you got it wrong. And tonight? What do you read in my being here, in your bed? Why do you think I made love with you, knowing that we've got to part?'

'I don't know,' he said sombrely. 'I'm confused. You came to me like a woman who loved me, and you gave everything. That's something I'm not used to. It's overwhelming. I know what I want to believe, but—' he searched her face with desperate anxiety '—I'm in your hands.'

Her mind was whirling. She could hardly take this in.

'I love you, Carson,' she said passionately. 'If you only knew how much I love you! But I thought she was still between us, that she'd left you empty and unable to love. I thought you wanted a mother for Joey and there was nothing in your heart for me but a little affection.'

'A little affection? My darling, if I could only tell you— Gina? What is it?'

She was rocking back and forth, her arms clasped about herself, laughing and crying together.

'What is it?' he asked again, alarmed by the wild note in her voice.

'I don't believe this,' she wept. 'How can we have found out now, when it's too late?'

With a groan he pulled her against him, burying his face in her hair.

'It mustn't be too late. You're my love, my only love. After this there can't ever be anyone else for me.'

'Truly?' she whispered, joyful in the midst of her anguish.

'With all the truth of my heart, I swear it.'

'But those things you said about what we had in common—you practically told me once that you only wanted a sensible marriage—'

'Maybe I thought I meant it, but I know better now. If we were just being sensible, my heart wouldn't be breaking at the thought of losing you. *Dear God, this can't be happening!* We can't have found each other, only to lose each other in the same moment.'

'But we can,' she said despairingly. 'Oh, my dearest, kiss me; kiss me again and again. If it's all we have—'

'It mustn't be. I won't let you go. Do you hear me? *I won't let it happen.*'

It would be so easy to yield to his insistence, and the temptation tortured her. It was unfair, she thought rebelliously, that the onus must be on her. But Joey's face was before her, and she hardened herself to do what must be done.

'For the moment, at least, you must give me up,' she said. 'You can't send Brenda away. It will break Joey's heart.'

'But we both know that her games won't last. She'll tire of it—'

'She'll go on as long as it's useful to her. Maybe long enough for Joey to grow older and cope better. Don't force the truth on him, Carson. He couldn't stand it.'

'Isn't it better for him to accept it now?'

She couldn't bear any more. Driven to desperation, she faced him with the situation in the bluntest, cruellest terms she knew.

'All right,' she said. 'Maybe he should be told that the mother he thought loved him is using him heartlessly, that his happy dream is over, and he's actually as rejected and abandoned as he feared. Will you tell him that, my darling? Or shall I?'

He seemed to grow older before her eyes as the inevitability of what she was saying sank in.

'You're right,' he whispered in horror. 'We can't do that to him. However much we reason around it, when it comes to the point—we can't.'

They looked at each other. There was nothing more to say.

Slowly he put his arms about her, drawing her close against him, not making love to her now, but needing to feel her warmth. They lay holding onto each other as the night passed and the first light of dawn crept in.

Gina watched it with bleak eyes. She'd told herself that in marrying Carson she was accepting second best, that the most she could hope for was a sedate, pedestrian love. Now she knew the glorious truth—that it was she and she alone whom he loved. She had his whole heart, his passion, his trust, his soul. She had everything she wanted.

And it was all too late.

As the light grew she asked herself whether it would have been better never to have loved him than to have known this pain. But her heart knew the answer. She'd had her moment of glory, and, however long it must last her, it would be enough to live on.

At last Carson said, 'I won't believe that this is the end. Some day we'll find each other again and, when we do, I won't have changed.'

'And nor will I. However far away that is, I'll still love you, just as I do now. Hold me. Hold me!'

She buried her face against him, her shoulders shaking. And he held her in silence.

* * *

Angelica confronted Gina in the kitchen while she was making coffee.

'Now I know who you are,' she said belligerently. 'It was you on the phone that time. I didn't recognise your voice at first. So you've been here ever since, worming your way in.'

'I was here to help Joey.'

'Nice try. You took a look around you and thought you'd get your hands on the goodies. I don't suppose a speech therapist, or whatever you are, earns very much.'

'I'm a lawyer.'

'Oh, a lawyer. But you just happen to have spent the last few weeks being a drudge in this place, and you expect me to think you're not on the make?'

'You can think what you like,' Gina said quietly.

'Oh, I'll do that. I know your sort. Thought it would be easy to take over another woman's home and husband. Well, think again, lady. I'm back to stay.'

Gina faced her. 'As long as you make Joey happy, that's fine.'

'Don't you lecture me about my son,' Angelica said viciously. 'I want you out of here, fast.'

'Don't worry. I'm going. But I'd like to talk to you about Joey first. There are things you need to know about his development.'

'Like what? He can hear, can't he?'

'In a way, but—'

'Well, you wouldn't know it. I can't understand a word that kid says. As for those signs—'

'You can learn them. Mr Page did.' Gina added bleakly, 'I'm sure he'll teach you.'

'But why should I have to learn them? I thought once he had that thing he'd be all right. But he's just like before. I suppose that's your doing.'

Gina looked at her sharply. 'What do you mean by that?'

'Oh, come on! That's how you got your feet under the table, isn't it? Poor little kid—needs you. You weren't going to let him be normal too soon, in case Carson wised up.'

Out of sight Gina clenched her hands, angrier than she'd ever been in her life. But she subdued her rage. For Joey's sake she must make this unpleasant woman face the reality of his condition.

'I won't answer that,' she said when she could speak calmly. 'But you have to know how things are for him.'

'All right, all right. Maybe later—'

'Shut up and listen!'

Angelica's jaw dropped. Nobody had talked to her like that for years. Taking advantage of her silence, Gina explained about Joey's implant, and about the time and work it would take before he could speak properly.

Angelica blew out her cheeks. 'Well, it's not what I expected, I'll tell you that.'

'Just be patient with Joey. He's learning fast, and now he's got you back he's—well, he's perfectly happy. If you'll just learn a few signs—'

'No way. That stuff gives me the creeps. If Joey can hear now, it's time he sharpened up his act. And he'll do it a lot better without you around, miss. So—out.'

There was a noise in the doorway and they both turned sharply to see Joey standing there. He was looking from one woman to the other and it was impossible to tell how much he'd followed. Angelica was in profile to him, making lip-reading difficult, and anything he'd heard would be no more than a jumble of sounds.

The actress gave her son an effusive greeting, which

made him smile. He began to sign, which made her mouth tighten.

'He said "Hello, Mummy",' Gina told her in a strained voice.

'Well, he can say it, then, can't he?' Angelica demanded.

'Let him do it when he's ready,' Gina begged.

'I told you to keep out of it, lady. He can speak properly if he wants to, and he'll be fine when he hasn't got you here holding him back.'

Her tone changed and she swooped on Joey again. 'Come along, darling. You can do it for Mummy, can't you? Now say it—Hello, Mummy.'

He tried. It was a good try for a child who'd only been able to hear for a few days, but not close enough to please Angelica. She winced.

'Never mind,' she said through gritted teeth. 'We'll try again later.'

Carson overheard part of this and it increased his sense of moving through a nightmare. Gina, who had taken every situation in hand and shown him the answers, seemed to have no answer for this.

The nightmare deepened with the discovery that Angelica had invited the press back that very day, determined to restage their reunion.

'If she thinks I'm going to allow that—' he growled.

'Let her,' Gina said. 'Sooner or later she's going to do this, and better now while I'm here to help Joey. After that, I'll have to go.'

'Have you explained that to him? He'll take it hard.'

'I'm not sure. I'm dispensable. I have a feeling that he may not even notice that I've gone.'

'After everything you've done for him—'

'Children are practical, darling. They take what they need to survive, and pass on.'

Joey was following his mother around, trying to communicate with her. When she didn't understand his signing he attempted speech, and managed some of the words. He didn't know that Angelica had expected to find all the problems solved.

He read her lips as she explained that they were going to have another party, some friends of hers would be coming and he must be on his best behaviour. He smiled, enjoying the thought of another party, but wondering when his mother would want to be alone with him so that they could talk, as they did in his dreams. As he talked to Gina.

He decided that Gina would know the answer to this, and went in search of her. He found her in her room, packing.

Where are you going?

'Back to my job, darling. That was what we agreed at the start—that I'd be here for just a few weeks.'

I don't want you to go.

'I have to. You don't need me any more. You've got Mummy now.'

Joey didn't react to this with the brilliant smile she'd seen so often on his face since yesterday. Instead he frowned and tilted his head in a considering manner, as though it was only just occurring to him that he couldn't have them both.

'You love your mother, don't you?' Gina asked gently.

His lip-reading seemed to fail him and she had to sign, crossing her folded hands on her chest to indicate 'love'.

Joey nodded, and now there was the smile. He understood that sign. It was what he felt for Brenda, Gina thought sadly. And that was how it should be.

He went away without communicating any more. Gina watched him go, with an aching feeling that made her angry with herself. What had she expected? The child had recovered his mother, and if Angelica's career really was on a downward slide perhaps she would be scared into behaving well. If not, Carson would know how to protect Joey. Everything was working out well.

Downstairs Angelica was getting agitated. She'd put on a glamorous dress and made herself up to kill. What was left of the cake had been wheeled out, and she was distributing the presents that she'd brought the day before. She frowned when she saw Joey.

'Why aren't you wearing the clothes I bought you? I don't want you in old jeans and a sweater.'

She spoke too fast for him and Gina, who'd followed him into the room, interpreted.

'For pity's sake!' Angelica muttered. 'Don't tell me he didn't get that. What is he, dumb or something?'

'No, he's exceptionally intelligent,' Gina said. 'But he couldn't see your lips and he doesn't know the words yet.'

'Well, get him into those things I brought. It's top-quality designer gear and it cost me a bomb on Rodeo Drive. What's he saying?' For Joey was signing something.

'The clothes are too small,' Gina explained. 'He's grown a lot recently. 'Does it matter what he wears?'

'All right. Leave it. But make him hold this.'

Angelica took up a football and pressed it into Joey's hands. 'You like football, don't you?' she asked.

He shook his head.

'Nonsense, of course you do. All kids like football.'

Carson entered the room, having overheard the last part of the conversation. 'He doesn't,' he snapped. 'It bores him. He's interested in marine life.'

'In what?'

'Fish, to you.'

'Well, if you think I'm going to let people see him holding a damned fish—! Of course he likes football.'

Joey shook his head.

'Yes, you do! All boys like football. That's how you know they're boys.'

Joey tried to explain, using words since she didn't understand signs. Angelica listened to the incoherent noises that came from his mouth, and she froze.

'Look,' she said, dropping down so that her face was on a level with her son's, 'I don't want you doing this. Just keep quiet. OK?'

But in his urgency to explain the child ignored her. His quick brain lined the thoughts up too fast for his mouth to cope with. Sounds poured from him in a jumble and he grew more and more agitated.

So did Angelica. She rose and tried to pull away from him, but Joey seized her arm, trying to make her listen.

'Yes—yes—' she said, struggling to maintain her smile and free herself. 'All right, all right, but not just now—careful—my dress.'

He couldn't follow. He held her more tightly and words poured from him. 'Mom-mee, mom-mee—'

In his agitation he didn't notice a tall glass of milkshake on the table. His sleeve brushed it, sending it flying, and next moment strawberry milk was sprayed over Angelica's beautiful gown.

'Look at me!' she screamed. She whirled on Joey.

'What's the matter with you, brat? *I thought you were supposed to be normal now.*'

Gina tensed at the look on Joey's face. He'd read Angelica's lips without trouble. He'd also heard her, not making out individual words, but sensing the malevolence in her tone.

In that moment Joey understood all about his mother, and his eyes filled with tears.

Gina began to edge carefully towards the child, letting him see her and know she was there, but not putting pressure on him. Young as he was, what happened next was for him to decide.

Angelica pulled herself together, evidently realising that she was ruining her own performance. Somehow she hoisted a fractured smile into place.

'I'll have to go and change, won't I? I've just got time before the press arrive.' She tried to sound ingratiating. 'You didn't mean to spoil Mummy's dress, did you?'

Joey didn't answer. He just looked at her.

'I hope you're not going to look so stupid when they're taking your picture,' Angelica snapped.

'Nobody's going to take his picture,' Carson said quietly. 'This farce is over. Get out of here, now!'

She gave him her gayest laugh. 'Why, darling, you don't mean that. What a fuss about a little blip.'

'I never meant anything more seriously in my life. Get your things together and leave.'

'Don't be silly. The press will be here any minute.'

'Yes, they will, and if you're still here I'll give them a story that will make your public look at you with new eyes.'

Angelica played her last card. Turning to Joey, she cried, 'You don't want me to go, do you, darling?'

He didn't answer, but stood looking at her steadily.

She raised her voice. 'You want me to stay. You love Mummy, don't you?'

Joey regarded her in silence for a long moment. Then he stepped close to Gina, and took her hand.

'Yes,' he said simply and clearly.

At first Gina wondered if she'd understood right. Surely Joey couldn't mean…?

Then she found him looking up at her, his eyes full of thoughts too old for his years. He had meant exactly that.

'You've had your answer, Brenda,' Carson said.

'Don't call me that!'

'I'd have put up with you for Joey's sake, but now that even he's seen through you you've got no hold on me any more. In fact, it's the other way round. You cause any trouble and I'll give the press a story that will finish your "image" for good, and destroy what's left of your career.'

Angelica visibly blenched. 'You can't do that. You mustn't—it's all I—'

'It's all you've got left,' Carson supplied. 'Yes. Once you had a husband and son who adored you but you threw them away. So now they've both chosen somebody else—a real woman, with a heart, that they'll both love as long as they live. Now go and pack. There'll be a taxi here when you come down.'

'You think you're so clever, the pair of you,' Angelica snapped. 'But I've still got friends. I'll tell them what you did to me, how you threw me out to make way for some speech therapist—'

'Lawyer,' Carson snapped.

'No,' Gina said quickly. 'Speech therapist sounds much better, doesn't it, Angelica? Someone who under-

stands Joey and can help him—which, as a loving
mother, is all that you want.'

'What?'

'You've been treated really badly,' Gina went on.
'You'll get a lot of sympathy when you tell the world.'

'Gina!' Carson exploded, but she held up a hand to
silence him. And he drew a sharp breath, for suddenly
he could see the knives flashing from her eyes.

'If you time it right,' Gina went on, 'the first interview
will appear the day Carson's divorce becomes final.'

'The *first* interview?' Angelica echoed slowly.

'I'm sure someone with your skill can get two bites
of the apple. Carson and I will be getting married in a
few weeks. I'll let you know the date, and you can give
another interview that will really spoil the day for us.'

That thought brought a smile of malicious pleasure to
Angelica's face. Gina watched it with contemptuous
pity. As though anything this creature could do would
spoil the day she became Carson's wife!

The eyes of the two women met. Somewhere in the
silence a deal was made.

'Of course,' Angelica said at last, 'for my child's sake
I'm ready to make the sacrifice—even if it means giving
up my husband and home...'

She spoke slowly because calculations were seething
through her brain. For a moment they could all see the
headlines that would proclaim her a martyred saint.

'And since neither Carson nor I are going to talk to
journalists,' Gina added, 'there'll be nobody to contra-
dict you.'

'You say that, but what about you?' She turned on
Carson. 'Does she speak for you?'

'Of course,' he said in disgust. 'Get out of my hair,

and I'll keep out of yours. I won't sell any fewer engines because of what you say about me.'

'But you and Joey must stay in touch,' Gina offered her quickly. 'In a while, when he can talk properly, we might visit you out there, and you and he can—'

Angelica swung around so that she was facing Gina and hidden from Joey.

'Get real,' she muttered. 'He's all yours.' To Carson she said, 'Make sure that taxi's there in ten minutes.'

She went upstairs. A few minutes later she had left the house without a backward look.

Joey watched his mother's departure in silence, staying close to Gina. He'd been hurt, but in another way he'd also come to the end of his hurt. Like his father, he had made his choice, and it was for ever.

When they were alone he tugged at Gina's hand.

You won't go away now?

'No, I'm staying always, darling.'

'I'm going to make sure of that,' Carson said.

Joey touched his father's sleeve, indicated Gina and put his hands together as if clapping, the fingers of one hand folded over the back of the other.

'I don't know that one, son.'

'It means marry,' Gina said huskily.

'Yes, we're going to marry,' Carson told him.

When?

'Next month.'

Joey made another gesture.

'That's right,' Carson agreed. 'We do—all three of us.'

'Did you understand that one?' she asked shakily.

'Yes, but only because you taught me. Without you, I might never have understood.'

'Do it, Carson. I've heard you say it, but I'd like to *see* you say it, just once.'

He nodded. Gravely he faced her, folded his hands and crossed them on his breast.

'Love,' he said.

It's hard to resist the lure of the Australian Outback

One of Harlequin Romance's best-loved Australian authors

Margaret Way

brings you

Look for

A WIFE AT KIMBARA (#3595)
March 2000

THE BRIDESMAID'S WEDDING (#3607)
June 2000

THE ENGLISH BRIDE (#3619)
September 2000

Available at your favorite retail outlet.

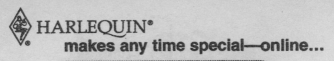

HARLEQUIN®
makes any time special—online...

eHARLEQUIN.com

shop eHarlequin

- Find all the new Harlequin releases at everyday great discounts.
- Try before you buy! Read an excerpt from the latest Harlequin novels.
- Write an online review and share your thoughts with others.

reading room

- Read our Internet exclusive daily and weekly online serials, or vote in our interactive novel.
- Talk to other readers about your favorite novels in our Reading Groups.
- Take our Choose-a-Book quiz to find the series that matches you!

authors' alcove

- Find out interesting tidbits and details about your favorite authors' lives, interests and writing habits.
- Ever dreamed of being an author? Enter our Writing Round Robin. The Winning Chapter will be published online! Or review our guidelines for submitting your novel.